# ''Miss, there is some question about your invitation.''

The security guards were very polite. ''Of course,'' Heather said, and fumbled in her tiny handbag, groping for time.

''Goodness, it seems to have disappeared. I wonder where—''

It was too late.

''If you'll come with us for a moment.''

Another minute and any possibility of getting Cole Dennison's attention would be gone.

''Dennison!'' she cried, and the voices of the startled crowd began to ebb away. ''Cole Dennison!'' Cole stopped and turned, and she had the minor satisfaction of watching his eyebrows shoot up.

The security guards lifted her off her feet and started for the ballroom door. Heather turned her head and shrieked, ''Damn it, Cole, you can't get rid of me as easily as this. What are you going to do about my baby?''

**Leigh Michaels** once baked a single cookie for a friend who was having a craving for chocolate chips, on the principle that one cookie couldn't hurt. (The cookie, however, was eighteen inches in diameter.)

Writing about Heather DeMarco's *Cookys,* with its multitude of rich and tempting concoctions, brought back her old urge to operate a cookie-baking shop. Common sense, however, tells her it wouldn't be a wise idea. "I'd eat up all the profits," she says.

## Books by Leigh Michaels

HARLEQUIN ROMANCE

3070—A MATTER OF PRINCIPAL
3086—AN IMPERFECT LOVE
3119—AN UNCOMMON AFFAIR
3141—PROMISE ME TOMORROW
3160—TEMPORARY MEASURES
3171—GARRETT'S BACK IN TOWN

HARLEQUIN PRESENTS

1107—CLOSE COLLABORATION
1147—A NEW DESIRE
1245—ONCE AND FOR ALWAYS
1266—WITH NO RESERVATIONS

# OLD SCHOOL TIES

## Leigh Michaels

Harlequin Books

TORONTO • NEW YORK • LONDON
AMSTERDAM • PARIS • SYDNEY • HAMBURG
STOCKHOLM • ATHENS • TOKYO • MILAN

ISBN 0-373-03184-X

Harlequin Romance first edition March 1992

OLD SCHOOL TIES



Printed in U.S.A.

# CHAPTER ONE

DUSK HAD COME early to Archer's Junction, for it had been drizzling for most of the day. The old-style streetlights that lit the business district were winking on, one by one, a couple of hours earlier than was normal for mid-April. Business had been slow because of the cold, unpleasant rain; the shop that specialized in Depression glass had already closed, as had the antique-lace store and the wrought-iron business.

Inside Cookys—in the narrow little storefront between Depression glass and antique lace, and across High Street from wrought iron—the lights were bright, and the aroma of raisins and chocolate and nuts still hung heavily in the air. But it was deceptive; Cookys smelled that way even in the early morning, before the first oven was turned on or the first batch of sweet dough was mixed.

Heather DeMarco picked up a small waxed paper bag, opened it with a professional flick of the wrist and sacked up a couple of double-chocolate-chip cookies for a late customer. At the cash register, Katherine DeMarco made change. Heather saw her yawn furtively.

"Mother," she said firmly, "go home. I'll take care of closing up tonight."

Katherine's second yawn wasn't so easily concealed. "I'm all right, Heather. It's just the weather, I think. When it rains like this all I want to do is crawl into my cocoon and sleep." But she didn't hesitate to trade her dark brown apron and cap for raincoat and umbrella, Heather noticed.

After Katherine was gone, she began to clear the cases, moving the leftover cookies down to the end cabinet so she could clean the rest. It was not her favorite part of the job, but after two years at Cookys, she could do it with her eyes closed.

Across the glass counter, a teenage boy—one of several who still lounged around a small table—looked up hopefully. "As long as you have to throw all those leftovers away, Heather," he began, "you might as well throw them to us."

She laughed. "You know the rules, Rod. Buy six and get one free."

He looked downcast. "Not even a special deal for me?"

"Stop on your way to school tomorrow and I'll make you a price. But they aren't day-old till tomorrow, so stop trying to talk yourself into a bargain now."

He grinned. "It was worth a try," he confided, and bought the last three oatmeal-pecan cookies in the case. "Sometimes your mother will make a deal."

Heather sacked the cookies up for him and said, "My mother is an easy mark. Now get out of here, all of you. It's quitting time. Besides, this is a business, not a hangout for the football team."

"My feelings are hurt," Rod complained. "I'm the least troublesome customer you have. My mother is actually grateful that you ruin my appetite with cookies every day before I come home for dinner." He pulled the door open. "But since we're obviously not wanted here, come on guys. Let's go up to the school and toss a basketball around."

Heather frowned. *It's none of my business,* she reminded herself. Nevertheless, she called, "Wait a minute, guys. You don't mean the old school, do you?"

Rod looked a bit sheepish, as if he wished he hadn't said it loud enough for her to hear. "Yeah."

Heather said carefully, "I thought it was supposed to be locked up tight."

Rod sounded a bit defensive. "We didn't break the padlocks off the door, Heather, somebody else did. But the fact is the locks are gone again, and so the building is standing there wide open. It's the only decent gym floor in this whole end of town, and it just sits there. What's so wrong with playing on it?"

"Because it's not a public school anymore. It's private property, Rod. And you're trespassing when you go in there without permission."

"So who's going to notice? Nobody ever pays any attention to it except the hoods who break off the locks. Why should they be the only ones who ever enjoy it?"

"That's beside the point, guys. It doesn't belong to you."

Rod was matter-of-fact. "If what's-his-name gave a damn about the building, he'd do something with it, wouldn't he?"

Heather bit her lip, hard. Rod was one bright young man, she had to grant him that. His line of reasoning mirrored her own conviction, and it was difficult to argue against herself.

Rod pressed his point. "It stands to reason that he'd turn it into something useful, or sell it to someone who would. Or he'd at least lock it up securely till he gets around to it. Those cheap padlocks—" He made a face. "My baby brother could break them off in two minutes flat. It's like the guy doesn't care who gets in."

"Rod, that doesn't excuse trespassing."

"Face it, Heather, he's never going to do anything with that place. It'll sit there and rot and one day the roof will fall in. So what's so awful about someone getting some good out of it in the meantime?"

It wasn't that she didn't have an answer, but the boys were gone by the time Heather found her tongue. She sighed unhappily and finished cleaning the display cases while she thought about her options. Should she call the local police station? The boys were clearly wrong, but surely turning them over to the law would be excessive. They'd no doubt be blamed for the break-in, and end up with criminal records over a simple basketball skirmish, while the real villains escaped altogether.

And she wasn't foolish enough to believe that would be the end of it. It had happened before, after all: someone in the neighborhood would complain to the corporation that owned the property, the building would be secured for a while, someone would break in again, and it all started over. She wasn't going to change that now by simply calling in the police. The only thing that would change was her relationship with the boys; if she reported them, she'd never have another ounce of influence over any of them.

*I'll talk to them tomorrow,* she decided. *And I'll tell them that if there's one more incident, I'll report them, no matter what.* She'd have to, because if one of them were to get hurt up there—

The thought gave her an uneasy ripple in the pit of her stomach. What if one of them got hurt tonight, and she could have stopped it?

*They may have been going up there every day for weeks, Heather,* she reminded herself. *The fact that you only found out about it doesn't mean it just started.*

She tossed her chocolate-stained apron into the laundry hamper, brushed out the stream of mahogany-brown hair that had been tucked up under her cap all day and started up High Street toward her apartment. Just a block beyond the retail district, the old school loomed up out of the evening dimness, off to her left on a gently sloping hillside. She stopped to look up at it with a dispirited sigh.

It was a heavy building, sitting squarely in the center of an entire city block. The sloping lawn between school and street had once been kept manicured, but now it was overgrown with weeds. The school's lower floors were native fieldstone, huge solid dusty-beige blocks, while the upper stories were built of oversize dark red paving brick. The windows and the entrance and the irregular roofline showed Gothic influence, with pointed arches and lacy stone trim that relieved the weight of the facade. Above it all a tower soared two stories higher yet.

In daylight, one could still see the beauty that remained in the brick and stone that had been so carefully crafted a century ago. But in the dim light of evening the old building merely looked tired and dilapidated and decrepit—like something from a bad gothic movie. All that was needed to complete the illusion, she thought, was a mist to cling around the lower floors, and a swarm of bats circling the high chimneys and the irregular peaks of the roof.

It looked dead, she thought, this old building that had served students for ninety years and then been discarded to stand empty for another five. Most of the glass panes had been either broken out or covered with plywood years ago. The few windows that still remained intact stared blankly out across the valley, and a couple of nearby streetlights reflected weakly off the dirty glass.

Those lights, dim as they were, must be how the boys saw to play basketball inside the wing that held the gym; she hadn't even wondered till now how they managed that in the dark old building, with the power shut off long ago. What a waste it was, she thought, to take a perfectly sound building and let it dwindle into a useless hulk!

"It's a sin," she said vehemently.

She wasn't aware that she had said it aloud until a man spoke behind her. "That's for certain."

Heather wheeled around to see an old man stooping over a small bush at the corner of the brownstone apartment house. "Oh... hello, Mr. Maxner. Isn't it a little wet to be planting things?"

"I'm not planting, Heather, just checking on the progress of what I put in last year. The forsythia is just starting to bloom, you know."

Heather glanced at the hints of yellow on the bush, and then at the sky. "It looks as if it will get another good drink before the night's out. Look at those clouds stacking up behind the school."

The old man stood up slowly and looked up at the building's silhouette, fading now against the darkening sky. "I got my education there, you know, and it's still a lot more solid than the so-called modern wonder they built to replace it."

Heather sighed. "I know. I was down at the new school just last week. Five years old and it's already got cracks in the walls, and meanwhile this one just sits here, useless." With determination, she turned her back on it. "Well, it doesn't do any good to fret about it, does it? Dennison Incorporated doesn't seem inclined to put it to any use."

Mr. Maxner shook his head. "Is that who bought it? Can't think why Cole Dennison wanted it in the first place, when the school board declared it excess property, if all he was going to do was let it set."

From the top of the hill came a shout, and Heather turned to see a couple of boys come scrambling down the clay slope from the school, half-running, half-tumbling through the weeds.

*It's happened,* she thought frozenly. *And I'm at least partly to blame, because I knew they were there, and I did nothing.*

One of them was shouting, but when she realized what he was saying it made no sense at all. *Fire?* Her eyes met Mr. Maxner's, and she saw her question reflected in his face. How could there be a fire in the school? There was no electricity and no natural gas supply.

Mr. Maxner hurried up the front steps of the apartment building toward the telephone, and Heather bounded across the street toward the white-faced boys. "Fire?" she demanded. "Did you build a fire in there? You idiots—"

"No," one of them gasped. "We're not stupid. We smelled smoke when we went in, so we went looking and—It's in one of the storerooms above the gym, Heather. Clear on the top floor. Somebody set it."

In the distance she heard the shriek of sirens leaving the fire station. "Where are the others?" she asked crisply. "Rod and Steve and Brian and Jay—"

"They're still up there, trying to put it out. We ran for help."

*"They're still up there?"* It was not much more than a whisper.

"Yeah. There were some extinguishers in the gym."

The first fire truck pulled up. A captain, already in heavy rubber garb, swung down off the back, and Heather ran to meet him.

When he heard about the boys, he muttered, "Oh, hell," and turned to shout to his crew. Then he smiled wryly down at Heather. "Can't say I'm surprised they're fighting it," he said. "It got away from them, no doubt." He was gone, shouldering an air pack, before she could correct him.

It seemed hours, but she knew it could have been no more than five minutes before the missing boys stumbled down the stairs, with a fire fighter guiding them. They huddled in a clump in a corner of the school yard, disheveled and covered with soot, watching the commotion with eyes red from smoke.

The neighborhood residents were gathering by then. A hundred people were milling around, anxiously watching the telltale puffs of smoke, and eyeing the boys, as well, with suspicion.

Heather went over to the uncomfortable little group. They looked at her morosely, and Rod muttered, "Just go ahead and say it."

"All right, I will," she said calmly. "You guys smell awful."

"They think we started it, Heather."

"Surely you're not surprised by that? I imagine you'll all have a nice chat with the fire inspector tomorrow. You—and your parents."

One of the boys gulped. He looked very young all of a sudden.

Heather pressed her advantage. "And next time you decide to be heroes, you might think about possible consequences first."

"Heroes?" Rod snorted. "We are, you know. They said if it had had another fifteen minutes' start the whole building would be going up in smoke."

That sent a chill down Heather's spine. But before she could even begin to think through all the implications of the fire breaking into the attics and through the roof, it was over—the blaze was out, and the danger was past. It had been a minor fire—if, she told herself glumly, there ever was such a thing as a *minor* fire. Archer's Junction had been lucky.

This time, she found herself thinking. But what about next time? For it was obvious that someone had set that fire on purpose, and equally obvious that it would not be difficult to do it again. And if, next time, no one happened to smell the smoke until it was too late . . .

The fire captain, supervising the cleanup, saw her shiver. "Young fools, trying to fight it," he said. "Derelict old buildings aren't worth the risk of a human life."

"But if they hadn't found it and tried to help—"

He shrugged and pulled off his helmet, wiping sweat from his forehead. "Then it could have been one hell of a blaze," he said calmly. "Fire could smolder in there for hours behind those sealed-up windows, and once it broke through the roof—" he waved a hand down the street "—with a stiff breeze, it could have taken out half the retail district, too."

"What a cheerful thought," Heather said. Her voice felt frozen.

"Just giving you the facts," he said coolly. "We'll leave a crew here to watch it for a while, of course."

She forced herself to smile. It certainly wasn't his fault. "Thank you—all of you. I'll bring up some cookies for them."

He was watching her closely. "Cookies? This really is a small-town kind of neighborhood, isn't it? I just transferred out here from the middle of the city, and believe me, no one there would bring cookies to the fire fighters." He touched his fingers to the wide brim of his helmet and climbed back onto the truck.

The owner of the antique-lace shop had been listening, too. "Another conquest, Heather?"

"The heck with Heather's boyfriends," snapped the owner of the wrought-iron place. "What about the fire? Do we just sit around like ducks in a row and wait for it to happen again?"

Heather swallowed hard. "No. No, we don't. I don't know what we do, but we aren't just going to wait. It's too important for that. I think, to start with, we should have a meeting of the neighborhood association. You're the president. You pass the word while I go put the coffee on."

"Right now?" The owner of the lace shop sounded doubtful.

"Why not?" Heather said briskly. "Right now is when we have the problem, isn't it?"

The wrought-iron lady rounded everyone up, and they squeezed into Cookys, twice as many people as the tiny store was designed to hold. They shared chairs, sat on the window ledges, leaned against the walls. They passed around foam cups of coffee until everyone was served, because there were too many of them even to form a line at the counter to serve themselves. And they talked, neighbor to neighbor, about the eyesore on the hill.

Heather was astonished at the outpouring of frustration. The closing of the school, and the transfer of its students to the new facility a few miles away in another suburb, had been a blow to the identity of the proud neighborhood. Once, Archer's Junction had been a fiercely independent little town, and it still resented being swallowed up by the exploding city. The big, empty school building looming uselessly over the retail district was a constant reminder of the way the little town's identity had been submerged in the metropolitan area. But what truly astounded her was the cynicism of the crowd. Nothing had been done in the past five years, they seemed to be saying, and nothing could be done about it now, either, so they would drink their coffee and have their say, vent their anger and then go off home as usual....

"Dammit," she said. It was just short of being a shout, and the buzz of multiple conversations died. "Something has *got* to be done. There's no reason we can't force Dennison to do something useful with that building."

Someone snorted. "Dennison? Nobody forces Cole Dennison to do anything. He's the one who does the forcing around this city."

"All right," Heather said impatiently. "So he's a tycoon. He's got money. He's got power. He's still only human."

There was a sardonic laugh from the back of the crowd. "There's been some debate about that."

Heather ignored the interruption. "If we go to him and tell him what's happening to his property—"

"D'you think he cares?" It was the man who ran the Depression-glass shop. "He owns half the city, Heather. He doesn't care about this little chunk of real estate."

"Then we make him care," Heather said stubbornly.

There was a murmur at that and a shaking of heads. "How? It could burn down or blow away and it wouldn't bother him."

"But it matters to us, so it's up to us to do something about it. Maybe we could sue him."

"That would be like a mosquito stinging an elephant," someone muttered.

"Make him mad enough," said another, "and he'll put us all out of business."

Heather put her chin up. "Oh, is that it?" she mocked. "You're afraid of a bully? How do you think bullies get to be that way, anyhow? It's because ordinary people cave in. Well, I'm not going to cave in. Are you with me or not?"

"Go get 'im, Heather," the wrought-iron lady said. "Let's take a vote, shall we? All those in favor of accepting Heather's offer to take up the matter of the school with Mr. Dennison, say aye. Those opposed—"

"That's not what I—" Heather began.

She was overridden ruthlessly by the wrought-iron lady. "I'd say the ayes have it. We'll hear Heather's report at the regular association meeting next week and discuss it further then. Adjourned!"

"I didn't exactly—"

But it was too late. The door had swung open under the ruthless press of people, and within minutes Heather was alone inside Cookys, gathering up the stacks of empty cups and wondering how she had managed to get stuck with the job of facing Cole Dennison. *Had* she volunteered?

She bit absentmindedly into a leftover caramel-coconut cookie, and ate half of it before she remembered she didn't really like the things. So she put the rest of it into the trash, turned out the lights and started for home.

Were her neighbors in the retail district correct? Was it a waste of time to talk to Cole Dennison? *They're crazy,* she thought. *Whenever there's a complaint about the school, he's taken care of it.*

*With the minimal effort,* she reminded herself. *It's hardly been an effective response.* And last fall when she wrote to him about the semiannual cleanup effort in Archer's Junction, she hadn't exactly seen hordes of lawn service people manicuring the school grounds. She hadn't got an answer at all, in fact, and spent a couple of days up there with a rake herself, making the place look a bit more presentable. And she'd probably have to do it again this spring....

But that was different, she thought. A little trash caught in the underbrush didn't threaten anyone's life and livelihood. Arson did.

*The man can't be a monster,* she reasoned. *If I can just point out to Cole Dennison what the inevitable end of this is going to be if it isn't stopped here, then he'll do something about it.* Anyone with good sense would, for his own self-preservation, if nothing else. And if there was one thing that everyone in the city agreed on, it was that Cole Dennison had a very lively sense of self-preservation.

She walked on up the hill with a lighter heart. She would show those cynics down in the retail district what could be done with just a little persistence!

IT TOOK more persistence than she would have believed just to get to talk to Cole Dennison's secretary, and when she did manage to get through, the woman told her she simply could not find a free minute in Mr. Dennison's calendar within the next three weeks. She sounded almost regretful; Heather thought she'd probably practiced the tone of voice.

Heather tugged impatiently at her skirt, which insisted on creeping up well above her knees. It was a narrow-cut apricot tweed, part of a brand-new spring suit, and far dressier than what she usually wore to work. She had put it on in case Cole Dennison could see her this morning.

*I don't know why I bothered,* she thought irritably. *Obviously I'll have months to get dressed for the occasion!*

"It's very important," she said firmly, before the secretary could disconnect her.

"Well, perhaps..." The woman sounded uncertain, and Heather's heart rose a fraction. "If you could tell me what this is in reference to, Miss DeMarco?"

"It's about a building he owns in Archer's Junction."

The secretary's voice warmed. "Oh, a building! Then you'll want to talk to Mr. Sheldon. That's what Mr. Dennison would suggest you do, anyway, so I'm glad we won't be wasting your time waiting for an appointment. I'll connect you with that department."

Mr. Sheldon's secretary had never heard of the old school in Archer's Junction. "Mr. Sheldon may know of it," she said helpfully, "but he's out of the office today. Oh, you say it's not a rental property? Then it wouldn't be our department at all. Perhaps Mr. Hanford in property management..."

Heather's head was swimming.

Mr. Hanford was actually in, and free to take her call. Heather dared to take a deep breath of relief as she started her story.

"A fire?" he said. "No, I haven't heard about that yet. It was juveniles, I suppose. Ought to be hung if they catch them, but then they never seem to. Well, fortunately it was only an empty building. Thank you for calling, Miss... Markley, was it? We'll certainly secure the premises."

"That's not what I—"

But Mr. Hanford had hung up. Heather drummed her nails on the side of the stainless steel refrigerator and said a few uncharacteristically pungent words under her breath.

Across the compact kitchen, Katherine took a baking sheet from the depths of an oven. "Heather, dear, it's not very ladylike of you to talk like that."

"Personally, I thought I was being mild, Mother. At least now I know who everyone's been talking to when they've complained about the school—and why they're so sure nothing will get done. Hanford is a—" She swallowed the rest of it and smiled at her mother. "And here I am taking it out on you, when you're doing me a favor by carrying all the load yourself today so I can see Cole Dennison."

Katherine's eyebrows rose. "I thought you couldn't get an appointment, Heather."

"I'll be back as soon as I can." She gave her mother a hasty kiss on the cheek, and shook a finger at her. "And by the way, I've been hearing tales about free samples after school, partner."

The accusation wasn't quite true, but it let her get out the door before Katherine could return to the real subject.

There were some situations, Heather told herself, where it paid to be vague.

Rush hour was over, so it took only twenty minutes to negotiate the freeways to the glass-and-steel heart of the city. It was one of the better things about living in Archer's Junction, Heather thought; one still had the advantages of the small town, with the city just on the doorstep. Actually, she seldom came downtown. If she couldn't find something in the shops in Archer's Junction, then the nearby suburban shopping malls were sure to have it.

But she certainly knew where to find Dennison Incorporated; everyone knew that. Just last year Dennison Tower had been completed, and it had opened with no end of pomp and fanfare. Heather had never been inside the tower, but she had seen it. The newspapers had made much of the fact that tons of marble had been specially quarried for the lobby, and that the huge panels of glass that sheathed the exterior had required an entirely new process of manufacturing.

She stopped on the sidewalk just outside the polished brass revolving doors and looked up. The sheer size of the place gave her the quivers.

*Don't think about that,* she told herself. *Think about the tremendous ego a man must have to build a monument more ostentatious than the pyramids, and name it for himself....*

She was surprised, after her experience on the telephone, that she didn't have to run a gauntlet of security to get to the executive floor; the young man at the information desk just directed her to the proper elevator with a smile. Heather smiled back rather weakly, and crossed the lobby slowly.

The seventy-fourth floor, she thought, and forced herself to take a deep breath, as she had been taught in the desensitizing class. *Close your eyes,* she instructed herself, *and think your way through it before you get on the elevator. You're in command of your body, after all. Being terrified of heights is a totally irrational emotion, and you can reason it away. You have to, if you're ever going to talk to Cole Dennison.*

She stood for a full minute with her eyes closed, and when she got on the elevator she was surprisingly calm. It helped, when she reached the executive suite, which had his name discreetly lettered on the door, to see that there were few windows—just walnut paneling, jewel-toned Oriental rugs, invitingly lush leather couches, an acre or so of pale gray carpeting and a secretary who looked every bit as cool as she had sounded earlier.

"Miss DeMarco to see Mr. Dennison," Heather said pleasantly.

The secretary frowned. "I don't believe I have—you called this morning, didn't you?"

"Yes. I spoke with Mr. Hanford about the matter this morning, but as it turns out, it is Mr. Dennison I need to see, after all." It was not a lie, Heather reminded herself. It was just carefully phrased, and if the secretary concluded that it was Mr. Hanford who had told her she needed to talk to the boss, well, that was all to the good.

The secretary looked doubtful. "If you'll have a seat—"

"Of course." She chose the nearest leather couch and tried to look immovable. Would they take her word for it? Or would they call Mr. Hanford? Maybe she'd be lucky, and he would have stepped out of his office....

The secretary picked up a notebook and walked across to a plain walnut door. Beside it was a discreet little keypad, and she pushed a series of numbers. There was a click and the panel slid open.

The man had to be locked in? Heather thought, a little wildly. Maybe he was some sort of monster, after all.

She got only a glimpse of the office beyond the walnut door before it closed with a soft swish behind the secretary, but she got the impression that it was huge and entirely bathed in sunlight. Of course, she thought, it would be a corner suite, probably with a stunning view of the city. *Well, I'll just stay away from the windows, that's all.*

The secretary returned to her desk. "He's very busy this morning. I don't know when he'll be able to fit you in."

"I'll wait," Heather said, trying not to sound breathless with relief.

But the minutes ticked by excruciatingly slowly, and nothing happened. Heather began wondering if it was only her imagination, or if the building really was swaying in the crisp spring breeze. Then she told herself not to worry about it; of course skyscrapers swayed when the wind blew, or they would topple. Great, she thought. That was just the encouraging reminder she needed!

So she concentrated on the secretary instead, watching her every move as she typed and filed and telephoned. The woman spent half an hour talking to what could only be a caterer, discussing petits fours and shrimp puffs and champagne for an upcoming cocktail party. From the sound of the arrangements, Heather speculated, the whole Third Army must be attending.

The secretary went back into the private sanctum; Heather watched thoughtfully, and this time saw an entire corner of the office, including what looked like a very good Impressionist painting above a marble mantel. She also saw—or thought she did—the combination of keystrokes that opened the walnut door.

*Fat lot of good that will do me,* she thought.

The secretary came back. "Mr. Dennison has left to keep a lunch appointment, I'm afraid. If you'd prefer not to wait—"

"Of course I'll wait," Heather said. *I'm certainly not going away,* she thought. *I'd never have the nerve to come up here again.*

But a few minutes later the miracle happened. The secretary picked up her coffee cup and went down the hall.

Heather was on her feet the instant the woman was out of sight. Her fingertips trembled as she reached for the keypad.

*I'll just sit down inside and wait for him,* she was thinking, *and the secretary will think I gave up. Obviously he went out some private way. He'll no doubt come back that way, too—and I'll be there. He'll have to listen to me for a minute, at least, and then I can get out of here.*

Her fingertips flicked over the numbers, hoping she was right, and she held her breath for one interminable instant until the lock clicked. She slid through the door almost before it was completely open, and tugged on it, trying to hurry its closing, for seconds that seemed like aeons. Then she saw the matching keypad inside and punched at it. Nothing happened.

"Beating on it isn't going to help, you know."

The voice came from behind her—calm, baritone, beautiful, every so slightly husky—and Heather wheeled around in something close to panic as a man rose from behind the desk. The sunlight streaming through the windows ten paces behind him made him nothing more than a silhouette.

His hand moved slightly at the corner of the desk.

"What are you doing?" Heather knew she sounded breathless and scared. "Calling up the security thugs to haul me out?"

"Oh, no. I'm sure I can handle you all by myself." The door slid shut behind her with no more than a whisper of sound.

"Do come in, Miss DeMarco," he said softly. "You wanted to see me badly enough to come bursting in here. Well, you have my full attention. Now what would you like to do with these precious private moments you've stolen for us?"

She was groping behind her back for a doorknob that she knew did not exist, as he started slowly toward her, tall and lean and threatening.

## CHAPTER TWO

"YOUR SECRETARY TOLD me you'd gone out for lunch," Heather said. It hurt to breathe; the oxygen stung her lungs as if it were ammonia fumes.

"And she told me that Joe Hanford had sent you over," the silhouette said calmly. "I happen to think the whopper you told is bigger than the whopper I told, Miss DeMarco."

She ought to have known she'd get caught, she told herself. She straightened her spine and put her chin up and looked at him as directly as she could, with the light dazzling her eyes. But she was certain that he knew as well as she did that her stance was nothing but bravado and would collapse at any moment.

"It was very foolish of you to tell that sort of lie, you know," he went on dispassionately. "It's far too easy to check out."

Cole Dennison crossed from the sun-drenched half of the office into the shadow, and for the first time she could see him clearly. It was not a comforting first glimpse; he was smiling, but it was a tiger's smile, she thought, as he surveyed his prey.

*DeMarco, you're an idiot,* she told herself. *Of course he's acting like a maniac, but he's got reason; you* did *get caught in the act of burglarizing his office. And the sooner you explain to him why you're really here—*

But her tongue was still three times its normal size. *All right,* she told herself. *Give him a calm, friendly, reassuring smile instead. That's what you need to do.*

She took a firm grip on what little poise she still had and forced herself to really look at him, at the way his almost-black hair curled just a little at the ends, as if he'd been too busy to get it cut. At his eyes, large and dark brown and liquid and surrounded by a thicket of black lashes. At the strong wrists and powerful forearms under the rolled-up sleeves of his white shirt. At the flat waist and narrow hips and long legs. At the brown, long-fingered hand that was reaching for her arm...

She had never before met any man who exuded such a strong sensual aura—or at least she'd never been so close to one. It wasn't his looks; she had known men who were, strictly speaking, far more handsome. It wasn't his clothes or his surroundings or his reputation, either. It must be chemical, she thought half-consciously. And not any commercial, carelessly applied variety, for she could smell his cologne, and that had nothing to do with it at all. It must be something he manufactured himself, some extra masculine hormone, perhaps.

She swallowed hard. "So you were just going to let me sit there and wait all day? For nothing?" It was supposed to be a challenge, but it came out rather weakly.

Cole Dennison shrugged. "I've found it is generally the most effective way to discourage...that sort of attention." The huskiness was back in his voice, a sort of suggestive softness.

It took a moment for Heather to see what he meant, and when she did, her jaw dropped. "You actually think I went to all this trouble in the hope of getting a glimpse of *you?*" It was almost a shriek.

"It does happen," he said softly.

"Maybe it does. I suppose there are women who find your sort attractive—or perhaps I should say your money. But *I* certainly wouldn't go out of my way for such an arrogant, ridiculously conceited—" She heard what she was saying, and stopped, horrified.

"Of course, if I had realized the lengths you were willing to go to see me in private, Miss DeMarco—breaking and entering among them—I'd have invited you in right away."

There was something in that slightly rough voice that sent ice up her spine, something that made her think of spiders, and webs, and unsuspecting flies. "I didn't break and enter. I watched your secretary work the combination."

"Oh? A little industrial espionage, then? Were you hoping to find something interesting lying around while my back was turned? Too bad for you, in that case, that I decided to have lunch in my office. Of course, it was lucky for me that I decided to stay," he added smoothly, as his hand closed gently on her elbow.

"You don't need to worry about protecting your secrets from me—"

"Oh, I'm not. It's just that most young women who pull stunts like this don't look like you. I'd hate to have missed that." As if he were refreshing his memory, Cole Dennison's gaze slid slowly down the length of her with warm appreciation in his eyes.

"I need to talk to you," she said uncertainly.

"Of course you do." It was soothing. "Come and sit down."

At least he didn't say come and *lie* down, she thought a bit hysterically. For a moment there, she had almost wondered . . .

There was a little lounge area in a sunny corner of the office, with a leather couch and a couple of chairs and a smoked glass coffee table. He guided her to the couch. It was deeper than it looked, and as she sank into it, Heather's narrow skirt slid up her legs at something approaching the speed of sound. She tugged at the hem with a feeble attempt at casualness, painfully aware that Cole Dennison hadn't missed an instant. It wasn't until she was sitting down that she realized she hadn't given the window—or the no-doubt-spectacular view that would send her phobia into overdrive—a thought.

"I believe Mata Hari had nice legs, too," he said, as he settled down beside her, just a little too close for Heather's taste. His body was turned toward her, with his arm on the back of the couch, his hand not quite touching the mahogany-brown hair that flowed down over the collar of her tweed jacket, but close enough that she could feel the heat of it against the nape of her neck.

"You're wrong, you know." The determined shake of her head set her hair shimmering. "I've got nothing to do with espionage. I wouldn't know an important document from a telephone book."

"Pity," he replied. "I've always wanted to kiss a real live spy."

Her eyes widened in shock, and she realized that he was staring at her mouth. *He looks as if he's hungry,* she thought, and licked her lips nervously. "And I'm not psychotic," she went on desperately. "I mean, I'm certainly not like the nut who used to pursue that movie star because she thought she was married to him in a past life."

"I hadn't heard of that twist," he murmured. "But it might have some interesting implications." The tips of his fingers touched the nape of her neck, fleetingly. It was like being stabbed with a needle.

Heather plunged on, as fast as she could. "I wanted to see you about business, and I had to take this way of doing it because of the ridiculous blanket of security you've got surrounding you."

"I don't think it's so ridiculous," he returned. "Or so effective, either. After all, if you cracked it—"

"It was a last resort, believe me. I want to talk to you about a school you own out in Archer's Junction."

His dark eyebrows arched perfectly, she noticed, with not a twist or a kink or a ripple. "A school? I own a school? No, I don't think so. Of course, if I actually made the sort of donations to my alma mater that the chancellor seems to think I should, they should probably give me a deed, but—"

She interrupted. "To be more accurate, it used to be a school. Now it's just a derelict old building, and in legal terms it's an attractive nuisance—"

"Are you a lawyer?"

"No, but it doesn't take formal training to know that if you don't do something about it soon, you're going to get sued."

"How kind of you to take my legal affairs to heart." It was soft, almost sultry. "Who's going to do the suing? You?"

"No—the parents of whatever kids get hurt in there. Or the people whose businesses are destroyed the next time an arsonist decides to set it on fire."

He hadn't moved a quarter of an inch, but in the space of a blink, the lazy relaxation was gone. "What do you mean, the next time?"

*Well, at least I've finally got his attention,* she thought. *And on business, not on my knees!* "It almost burned to the ground yesterday."

"I haven't heard anything about a fire at any of my properties. I think you've got the wrong man, Miss DeMarco. I don't own—"

"Of course you own it," she snapped. "Your name is on the tax records. Besides, I sent you a letter a few months ago asking you to clean up the place, so you must know about it."

He shook his head. "That sort of letter would have been routed—"

"I know," Heather said in disgust. "To Mr. Hanford in property management! Well, ask him about it—he certainly recognized the place when I talked to him this morning."

He sounded amazed. "You really did talk to Joe? He told me he'd never heard of you."

"That's because he thinks my name is Markley. And I'm not surprised you haven't heard about the fire. I didn't expect he'd rush right in to tell you about it, because he didn't think it was important at all. That's why I insisted on talking to you."

The corner of his mouth twitched a little at that, but all he said was, "Tell me why you're so worried, Miss DeMarco."

She was startled. She knew she sounded angry, frustrated, annoyed—but she hadn't expected that someone like Cole Dennison would pick up so quickly on the fact that she was, above all, worried.

She told him about the fire, and the fire captain's prediction of the damage if it happened again under less-lucky circumstances. She told him about the blank, forlorn look of the old school as it sat there on the hillside, a discouraging drain on the entire neighborhood. She told him about the inadequate locks, and the vandals who kept prying them off. "For all I know, it's a gang hangout, too," she finished with a shrug. "The ones I'm really concerned about are the good kids who go up there to play basketball in that dark old gym—"

"What do you expect me to do about it? Put armed guards around the building to keep everyone away?" His voice was a marked contrast to the soft touch of his fingers against her neck.

"You'll be liable if one of those kids gets hurt, won't you? I'd think you'd be doing everything necessary to protect yourself from that."

"You do have a point there, Miss DeMarco."

She was taking a breath to add that if the building was put to some use, the problem would solve itself, when he moved abruptly across to his desk and picked up the telephone. "Maggie, is Joe back from lunch? I want him in my office the moment he gets back. Tell him to bring along anything he might have on—" He raised an eyebrow at Heather, and repeated what she said. "The former Noah Webster School in Archer's Junction. And I mean immediately. I want to move on this before the day is out." He put down the telephone and added, "There, Miss DeMarco. If it's our problem, we'll take care of it."

Heather shook her head in disbelief. "*If* it's your problem? You honestly don't know everything you own?"

"Well, we bought a company last year that owned a lot of strange bits of property, so I suppose it could have been one of those. But I still think you're mistaken."

"Believe me, I recognized the name on the tax records. There can't possibly be two of you, Mr. Dennison." She stood up and smoothed her skirt.

He watched, and then came across to her. "If it's not ours, I'll find out who does own it and let you know."

"Thank you." She turned at the door to offer him her hand, though she didn't really want to. He had at least turned down the charm; that was some relief, but the sensual magnetism was still there, just under the surface, and when his fingers closed around hers, it felt as if a million tiny feathers were brushing across her skin.

He didn't let go. Instead, his left hand came to rest lightly on her shoulder.

Heather looked up in surprise, her lips parted to ask what on earth he thought he was doing—and so it was not like any ordinary kiss at all. That sensual aura of his surrounded her in waves and seemed to hold her paralyzed. So her lips stayed moist and soft and willing under his, and it seemed very natural indeed when his tongue claimed the depths of her mouth, firm and strong and confident.

He released her slowly, as if he were reluctant to do so, and Heather blinked twice and said, "Why, you—" At least, that was what she tried to say; her voice had a strange kind of quiver in it, and the words didn't come out straight at all.

Cole Dennison smiled then. It was the first truly genuine amusement she had seen him display, and it took away what little breath she still had command of, for his whole face was alight with it—his eyes glowed, and there were funny little laughter lines everywhere and an amused sort of ripple in his voice. "You'd make a *good* spy, Miss DeMarco." It was an unrepentant murmur.

So she didn't try to slap him; it would obviously have been a waste of effort. Instead, she folded her arms across her chest and stared pointedly at the door. "Will you let me out, please?" she demanded, when he showed no sign of getting the message.

"Surely you don't need my help." But he smiled, and his fingers danced over the keypad, and the door slid open with a swoosh.

His secretary glanced up with a smile, saw Heather and dropped her coffee cup. She grabbed blindly for something to mop up the spreading brown pool on her highly polished desk.

Heather walked past, as fast as she could, and was already at the door when, from the corner of her eye, she saw Cole Dennison shake an admonitory finger at the woman.

"Better see about improving that entrance code, Eileen," he said. "I've been in moral danger for the past half hour."

Moral? Heather wondered. Surely he'd meant to say *mortal*. Hadn't he?

BUT A COUPLE of days—and a good ten miles' distance between her and the disturbing Mr. Dennison—restored both Heather's perspective and her sense of humor. It hadn't been so bad, after all. Cole Dennison had turned out to be no monster; he was a bit too self-confident, perhaps, and a little too certain of his own attractiveness, but at least he had listened to her.

And the man was efficient, too. On the very day after that crazy encounter in his office, she received a huge and brilliant bouquet of daffodils and tulips. The card said simply, "Mine. All mine." His name was scrawled carelessly across the bottom. Heather laughed and put the flowers on the wide ledge under the front window at Cookys, without bothering to take out the card.

The next day, when she walked to work in the still-dim morning, she saw an unmarked van pull up in front of the school. By the time she passed, there were people all around the building. Architects? she wondered dreamily. Engineers? Rehabilitation experts? Maybe now they'd really see some action!

The wrought-iron lady came in on Thursday to get her usual midafternoon snack—a seven-layer fudge bar and a cup of decaffeinated coffee with artificial sweetener—and looked at the flowers in the window with something close to shock in her eyes. "What does your mother think of this, Heather DeMarco?" she demanded.

"Nothing." Heather looked up from the freshly baked batch of double-chocolate-chip cookies that she was arranging in the case. "She's gotten flowers once or twice in her life, too."

"With suggestive cards like this one?" The wrought-iron lady snapped her fingernail against the pasteboard. "You must be a lot better friends with the tycoon than you've been letting on if he's claiming you."

Heather laughed. "Oh, no. He didn't even know where to send the flowers."

The wrought-iron lady snorted. "They got here, didn't they? I'd say he knew enough, then."

"They were addressed to 'Miss Heather DeMarco, somewhere in Archer's Junction.' And believe me, it's nothing personal. He just means the school belongs to him." But Heather moved the vase into the kitchen, and put the card in her pocket. There was no sense in letting stories get started, she thought.

"Was there any doubt of it?"

"Hard to believe that he could misplace a square block, isn't it? But he's going to do something about it, at least." The oven timer chimed and Heather removed a pan full of almond crisps.

"Well, I guess I don't care how you worked it. You got the job done, Heather. And promptly, too. They're unloading a couple of bulldozers up there right now."

Heather dropped the pan, and the cookies shattered all over the tile floor. "What do you mean? Bulldozers? They can't tear it down!"

"Well, I'm no keener than you are about a vacant lot growing up in weeds, but once it's cleared, maybe somebody will want to build there." The wrought-iron lady gathered up her snack and left the store.

The vague hope of future development was no comfort to Heather. She was trying to pull off her apron, but her fingers didn't seem to want to work anymore.

*I'll take care of it,* Cole Dennison had said. Well, if his method of taking care of it was to destroy a perfectly good old building...

She'd been so preoccupied she hadn't paid any attention to the man who had just come in. "Miss DeMarco? I came to thank you."

Heather looked up in astonishment. It was the fire captain; he looked much younger without the helmet and boots and protective rubber coat.

"It was very thoughtful of you to bring all those cookies to the fire station yesterday."

*Of all the moments to appear,* she thought. *Yesterday, I was disappointed that he wasn't there when I took the cookies over. I was going to tell him, so proudly, that I'd single-handedly prevented any future fires in the school.*

She certainly had, she reminded herself. Fires, and everything else as well. Because all that was going to be left was a pile of rubble.

"You're welcome," she said shortly.

He looked a little disappointed at the abrupt tone. "I brought you an official fire boosters hat," he said, sounding half-embarrassed. "It's the kind of thing we give the kids when they come to visit the station." There was no response, and he went on halfheartedly, "It's silly, I suppose, but I thought you might get a kick out of it."

She gave him the biggest smile she could manage. "Thanks. It's awfully sweet of you. But I have to go now." She tossed her apron and cap into the back room and grabbed her coat.

He was still standing in the middle of the store, holding the silly plastic hat and looking so downcast that she couldn't stand it.

"Oh, please," she said helplessly. "I'm not trying to avoid you, Captain, but they're starting to tear down the school—"

His face brightened. "And you want to be there to watch it go down?"

"I don't want to watch them destroy it. I want to stop them!" She practically pushed him out the door and pulled it shut behind them, her haste making her clumsy with the lock.

"What? That's ridiculous. An old firetrap like that—"

"But it doesn't have to be a firetrap. It just needs to be used! Am I the only one who can see that?" She started off up the hill at a breathless pace, leaving him behind.

Rod and a bunch of the other boys were watching from Mr. Maxner's front yard. "I thought you'd be over there in the thick of things," Heather said to them.

"We had to promise the fire inspector that we'd stay away from the place," Rod told her. "He believed we didn't set the fire—especially after what you told him about what good kids we were—but he said we'd better be prudent and keep our distance."

"Well, nobody's going to accuse you of destroying it this time, that's sure."

The breeze was cold on the hillside; Heather jammed her fists into her coat pockets and tried to figure out what was going on in the school yard. Her worst fears were not materializing, at least not yet. There was certainly a bulldozer in the parking lot, and another still on the flatbed trailer that had hauled it in. But there was no apparent damage to the building. She had been half-afraid that they would begin instantly, by driving headfirst into a wall.

She waited till the second bulldozer had backed cautiously down the ramp, and then she crossed the street and began to shout at the driver. He waved her away, parked the 'dozer beside its fellow and climbed down. "Yes, ma'am? You ought to stay back farther, you know. These old buildings crumble in funny ways, sometimes."

Heather didn't even want to think about that. "When are you going to start?"

"Oh, you won't see anything fancy till the crane gets here with the wrecking ball. You might want to come by in the morning to see the exciting part. They'll take the tower off first. Should have it all down in a few days. Of course, it'll take a week or two for the cleanup." He touched two fingers respectfully to the brim of his hard hat. "But stay back across the street where it's safe, you hear?"

A dump truck wheeled into the lot, followed by another flatbed carrying some kind of bucket loader. Two men began setting up barricades at the edges of the property and stringing plastic tape between them—the kind that police used to cordon off a crime scene.

How appropriate, Heather thought. Her eyes started to sting with tears. Cole Dennison was efficient, all right, she told herself bitterly. Too damned, bloody efficient! If the building was causing a problem, the answer was obvious to him. Remove it—and do it so quickly that there wouldn't be time for anyone to make a fuss. It would be gone before anyone could reach him to complain, that was sure. There could be a delegation waiting in his office for him tomorrow morning, but by the time they got in to see him, it would be too late to reverse the bulldozers' actions. He would, no doubt, make certain of that. There was no time....

Heather shook her head impatiently, trying to dispel panic and think calmly. *There has to be something I can do.*

The work on the barricades was going slowly; it would take a couple of hours to surround the whole block, she concluded. And then surely they'd have to walk through the place, checking each room and closet and corner; they couldn't just start knocking down walls without being sure that no one was inside, could they? And even if the crane arrived in the next few minutes, it would take time to set it up. Surely by then it would be the end of the working day, and the crew would knock off and go have a beer and come back in the morning and start fresh. Wouldn't they? Surely even Cole Dennison wouldn't have thought the matter was so critical that they had to work through the night. At any rate, they hadn't brought any lights, so they couldn't...

*So what good will that do you, Heather?* she asked herself. *You'll have the whole night to work out a plan and no time to put it into action!*

If only she could catch Cole Dennison somewhere tonight. If she could talk to him for just five minutes—

*Don't get your hopes up,* she cautioned herself. *Talking to him would probably be a waste of breath. If you're smart, you'll just throw a party tonight, Heather—a wake for the old school.*

Party, she thought. What was it about a party that nagged at the back of her mind?

Even if she could find him tonight, she told herself, it probably wouldn't change anything. But at least then she could tell herself that she'd tried with everything in her power to stop it.

*Party*... The nagging memory snapped into place, and she marched back across the street and up to Rod. "Do you want to see the school torn down?" she asked baldly.

"Well, it's going to be kind of exciting—"

She glared at him.

"That's not the answer you had in mind?" he asked. "What do you want, Heather?"

"Stay here till dark, Rod. Make sure they don't damage the building, and—"

"How am I supposed to do that?" he yelped. "Those are bulldozers!"

"You'll figure it out. Get inside—"

"Can't. They locked it up good and tight this time."

"Then chain yourself to the front door. Just give me a little time to get the demolition stopped."

"I promised the fire inspector I wouldn't hang around here anymore." But he was wavering. "I guess I owe you one for bailing me out with him, don't I?"

Heather restrained herself from agreeing. She said craftily, "Rod, I'll bake a whole batch of oatmeal-pecan cookies tomorrow, just for you." She was off before he could argue, flying down the street toward the brownstone apartment house on the corner.

*Party,* she was thinking. The cocktail party she had heard Cole Dennison's secretary setting up was tonight, at the downtown hotel he owned, and a party on that scale certainly couldn't have been the secretary's own. He'd have to be there, wouldn't he? It was Heather's best—probably her only—chance to get a word with him. And she had to try; he was the only man who could stop this devastation.

Which left her with just one big problem, she told herself with more confidence than she felt. What on earth did an uninvited guest *wear* to a cocktail party for hundreds?

IT WAS NOT MUCH easier to crash a party at Cole Dennison's downtown hotel than to get into his office, she concluded a couple of hours later. She hadn't been refused admission, because she hadn't yet tried to get in. But she had been drifting around the main lobby of the Palace

Grande long enough to know that no one was being admitted to the party without showing an invitation card and having his or her name checked off against a pages-long guest list. The security guards were posted at the bottom of the curving grand staircase that led up to the mezzanine ballroom, so no one could slip by.

Then a statuesque young woman in a floor-length dark mink coat and a gold tissue turban topped with a sort of spangled starburst appeared at the main entrance. Heather thought uncharitably that the headdress made her look like the lead horse in a circus parade. The splendor of the costume also made Heather's black cocktail dress look rather ordinary by comparison. But then, she reminded herself, she didn't want to stand out from the crowd, and obviously the circus horse did.

"Good evening, Mrs. Winchester," one of the security guards said. "It's nice to see you home again." He did not check the guest list.

The young woman looked down her nose at him as if deciding if the comment was worth responding to. The nose, Heather thought, rather added to the equine resemblance.

From behind Heather, a feminine voice shrieked, "Elizabetta Winchester! Oh, darling, it's so nice to see you! How was the Riviera?" A cloud of young women in a rainbow of colors swooped down around the circus horse and bore her up the stairs toward the ballroom.

Instinct pushed Heather into the fringes of the group, just in time to hear one of the women near the front tell the security guard who was posted at the ballroom door, "Oh, don't be such a fusspot. We've all just been to the ladies' room, for heaven's sake. The ones inside the ballroom are too terribly crowded."

And she was in. She promptly put as much distance as she could between herself and the group of women; she suspected from the cultured, flat accents that they all knew one another from some elite boarding school, and Heather didn't think she could manage to pass as one of them for long. So she snagged a champagne glass from a passing waiter and found a pillar in a secluded corner. She leaned against the far side of it and pretended she had been there all evening.

She had obviously misunderstood the secretary's arrangements; the affair was even grander than the elaborate cocktail party she had expected. The huge chandeliers were brilliantly lit. Across the room was a lavish buffet, with half a dozen ice carvings—of everything from a swan to a rearing unicorn—spaced along its length. On a central platform, an orchestra was playing. A handful of people were dancing, but most were milling around sampling the buffet or seated at the small tables that were grouped around the polished dance floor. The ballroom was so huge that it didn't seem crowded, but there must have been eight hundred people already there, and a steady stream was still flowing in.

She was surprised at how quickly she spotted Cole Dennison. He was not the tallest man there, nor the most distinctive in appearance, but it was only a couple of minutes before she found her gaze following a dark-haired man in a perfectly tailored plain black tuxedo, as he crossed the room from the bar to the big double doors—where Heather herself had been standing just an instant ago.

*It's that chemical magnetism of his,* she thought. *It's a good thing he's all grown-up—he'd be at a terrible disadvantage at hide-and-seek.*

He came up behind the woman with the gold tissue turban, and his hands rested on her shoulders. Heather saw her startled jump from across the room, and was a little surprised. He kissed the woman's cheek, and tenderly removed the mink coat from her shoulders. The dress underneath was entirely gold tissue, too, Heather noticed, long and sleek and shimmery, as if she intended to be the center of attention tonight. Well, she was certainly the center of Cole Dennison's attention—or was she? He was moving away.

*He's taking her coat to the checkroom,* Heather thought. *The special one inside the ballroom, where it will be safe from ordinary hotel guests. Well, if that isn't a sign of devotion!*

She pushed herself away from the pillar. If she could just get across the ballroom, she could ambush him at the checkroom window, and no one else would even notice.

The crowd had moved in her direction, and it was difficult to work her way through the streams of people. She stepped on someone's foot and looked up to murmur an apology, straight into the eyes of Cole Dennison's secretary.

Dammit, Heather thought. Eight hundred people, and she had to walk straight into the one who knew she had a habit of gate-crashing!

She ducked away, hoping the woman hadn't recognized her, hoping to lose herself in the crowd. She had almost made it to the checkroom when she saw the security guards closing in on her. Like all the guests, they were wearing evening clothes, but Heather's guilty conscience told her who they really were. There were only two of them, but they were big men, and they looked discreetly determined. They were coming at her from different directions, too—in order to cut off her escape, she supposed. She would be swept up and out the door, and no one would see a thing, except perhaps that one of Cole Dennison's guests had had a bit too much to drink, and had been taken out for some air.

The guards came to a halt less than two feet from her. "Miss, there's some question about your invitation," one of them said politely. "If we could see it, please?"

"Of course," Heather said, and fumbled in her tiny black handbag, groping for time. But she couldn't look long; it was only an evening bag, big enough for a comb, some change, a hankie and keys and not much else. "Goodness," she said with a nervous laugh, "it seems to have disappeared. I wonder where I could have dropped—"

It was too late. The mink was already safely entrusted to the personnel in the checkroom, and Cole Dennison was gone. From the corner of her eye, she could see him moving toward the buffet table, his hand on the elbow of the lady in gold tissue.

"If you'll come with us for a moment, we'll be happy to check the master list for your name," the other guard said, and a hand closed gently on each of her elbows.

They could lift her off the floor without a bit of effort, Heather realized. Another half a minute, and any possibility of getting Cole Dennison's attention would be gone. His back was toward her; he would not see, even if they carried her out. He would not even know she'd been there, until tomorrow when his secretary told him. Or perhaps next week sometime, when the security report on her might cross his desk. Long before then the school would be gone, only dust and rubble remaining....

She opened her mouth, intending only to let loose with the loudest scream she could manage. Where the words came from she did not know.

"Dennison!" she cried, and the voices of the startled crowd began to ebb away around her. "Cole Dennison!"

He stopped and turned, and she had the minor satisfaction of watching his eyebrows shoot up at a very unattractive angle.

The security guards lifted her off her feet and started for the ballroom door, and Heather turned her head and shrieked, "Dammit, Cole, you can't get rid of me as easily as this, you know! What are you going to do about my baby?"

## CHAPTER THREE

THE LAST THING Heather saw in the ballroom was Cole Dennison's dark head, bent over the woman in gold tissue as if to shelter her from the fallout of this madwoman's ravings—or as if he expected the ceiling to cave in next.

There was a sick feeling in the pit of Heather's stomach, and it wasn't all coming from the less-than-gentle way she was being carried, with a guard's hand clamped on each of her upper arms, and the rest of her body swinging because of the speed at which they were removing her from the ballroom. What on earth had made her say anything so ridiculous? Even if she had had to get his attention, why—for heaven's sake—had she said *that?*

Less than sixty seconds later she was firmly placed in a straight chair in a nearby anteroom. "Bruisers," she muttered resentfully, feeling vaguely that a frontal attack was the only route left open to her. She started to rub the abused muscles in her bare arms. "Look at this, would you? I won't be able to wear a sleeveless dress again for weeks till these marks fade."

The door opened. "DeMarco, you're getting to be a real pain in the neck," Cole Dennison announced. "Just what the hell is your problem tonight?"

One of the security men stepped in front of him. "Be careful, Mr. Dennison. We haven't checked her for a weapon."

Cole Dennison looked over the man's shoulder at Heather. His gaze slid slowly and intimately over her body, from the plunging neckline and spaghetti straps of her black dress, down to the irregular hemline of the gauzy skirt, to the toes of her satin sandals, and back up. By the time he was finished Heather was burning with embarrassment and fury. How dared he look at her like that, so obviously imagining what lay underneath?

"And just where would she be carrying a weapon?" he said derisively. "That dress certainly leaves no room for anything but her." He jerked a thumb toward the door, and the two men left—reluctantly, Heather thought.

Cole Dennison pulled a chair around, straddled it and folded his arms across its back so his wristwatch was in plain view. "You've got sixty seconds to explain yourself," he said.

She took a deep breath. "You can't tear that building down."

He hit the heel of his hand lightly against his temple. "Am I hearing straight? Dammit, you *wanted* it torn down!"

"I said it was an eyesore and a nuisance and that somebody would get hurt if you didn't do something."

"I'm doing something. I'm tearing it down, so it won't be an eyesore and a nuisance—"

"You can't tear down a landmark!"

"And you can't have it both ways, DeMarco! Which is it—a national treasure or a dump? It's had a damned fire in it—"

"It really wasn't a very bad fire," Heather said hopefully. "Even the inspector said it was minor, as fires go."

This time he rapped both sets of knuckles on the top of his head. "What the hell are you, anyway? One of those architectural historian types whose biggest pleasure in life is making a developer miserable?"

"I like old buildings," she said stiffly. "And this is a great old building. Have you ever seen it?"

"Why should I?"

"Because it's unique and interesting and solid and full of potential—"

"Also, no doubt, full of vermin and termites and problems just waiting to attack the unwary—"

Heather shook her head in dissatisfaction. "I don't think so. Is that what your architects and rehab people said when they looked at it?"

"What architects and rehab people?"

"The ones you sent over," she said, as if she were talking to a rather slow child. And then she realized what he was saying. "Do you mean that's not what they were?"

"They were demolition engineers, studying the safest and most efficient way to take it down."

Heather's voice rose into a screech. "You just sent the demolition crews in without even considering other options?"

"Miss DeMarco, this is a ninety-five-year-old building that was closed because it was outdated and inefficient. It seems to me that there aren't a lot of other options."

"It could be adapted for all kinds of possible uses!"

"Do you know what that sort of work costs?"

"You don't have to make a profit on everything, Dennison!"

He looked at her for one long moment, his index finger tapping his temple. "I have a headache," he announced.

"I don't wonder, beating yourself on the head like that."

"Talking to you is beating myself on the head," he muttered.

Heather thought it was better not to pursue that topic. "Besides, you'd have the joy of knowing you'd saved a landmark."

"I think I can survive the loss of self-respect I'll suffer by destroying it."

"Then why don't you let someone else have a chance to save it? It's a sin to tear it down."

"Are you making me an offer on the building?"

Heather looked around, not quite certain he could be talking to her. "I certainly don't have any money."

"Believe me, it wouldn't take much to get me to sell it. Of course, it's only fair to warn you that it would cost quite a few millions to put it back into shape." He checked his watch and stood up. "Your sixty seconds are more than up. Thank you very much for your concern about my property."

Heather stood, too, a little shakily. "You're going to go ahead, aren't you?"

"I haven't seen anything that convinces me to stop."

"Not even the building. Won't you come and see it, at least?"

"There's no point in it, Miss DeMarco. It would be a waste of time." His voice was gentle enough, but she knew there was no arguing with the trace of iron underneath.

She sniffed a little and rubbed the end of her nose, which itched. "What are you going to do with the site?"

"That's really not your concern, is it? You're free to leave, by the way. I'll put you straight into a taxi myself."

"I have my car," she said stubbornly.

"In that case, I'll have a security guard wait with you while the valet goes to get the car. Oh, I almost forgot." His tone was faintly ironic. "My congratulations about the baby. I do hope you're going to name it after me—I'll be so proud."

And he was gone before she could take off her shoe and use it to give him a headache he'd never have forgotten.

IT WASN'T QUITE DAWN yet, and Heather hadn't slept at all. She finally gave up on the idea of rest and climbed out of bed. She dragged a blanket out to her living room and settled herself on the wide ledge in the bay window. Her small apartment took up half of the second floor of the old brownstone building, and from her living room she had the best view in town of the old school.

Not for long, she told herself.

In the dim gray light of early morning, the building didn't look ominous, or haunted, or threatening. But the pride she had always been able to see in it—in the straight chimneys, the arched entryway, the soaring tower, the jaunty points of the window caps on the top floor—was gone. The old school was simply forlorn, standing there on its hillside alone, waiting hopelessly for the ignominious end that would come with the morning sunshine.

The moon had set long ago, and the low clouds in the eastern sky were beginning to glow as the early sun burned its way through. But down below, there were stars in the school yard....

She blinked and looked again. No, not stars, but lights—flashlights and lanterns, and here and there a flicker that could only be a candle's flame. There were people in the school yard, carrying lights.

She pulled on a pair of jeans and a sweatshirt and tore down the stairs. The door of Mr. Maxner's ground-floor apartment was open, and he was standing by the kitchen stove with the old enamel coffeepot in his hand. "Is it time, then?" he called as Heather went by. "For the stand-in, I mean."

"For the *what?*"

He laughed rustily. "That's what young Rod is calling it. It would be a sit-in, he says, except it's too cold to sit on the concrete over there. The boy must have spent half the night rounding up the neighborhood."

"The whole neighborhood?"

"A good part of it," Mr. Maxner qualified. "Nobody much likes the empty building standing there, but it seems they also don't like the idea of it being torn down in such a hurry. They feel like they should have something to say about it, or at least know what's coming next."

"So they're going to block the bulldozers?"

"Link arms and form a human fence around the whole building—I guess that's the plan. I'll be over in a while to help out." He sounded as excited as a kid himself. "I'd go now, but I don't want to tempt my rheumatism by being out in the wind any longer than necessary. Here—take some coffee with you. It's cold out there." He splashed some of the black brew into a stained old mug and handed it to her.

The group that had gathered in the school yard was not of the magnitude that had flocked to the cocktail party at the Palace Grande last night, but the demonstration might turn into just as interesting an event, Heather thought. It was certainly a crowd that couldn't fail to get Cole Dennison's attention.

The young woman who owned the antique-lace store was there, one hand cupped over her candle's flame, trying to keep it from blowing out in the crisp breeze. "I've always had this crazy dream of seeing the school turned into condos," she confided, "and getting the commission to put lace curtains in all the windows!"

Even the wrought-iron lady was there, though she was shaking her head in astonishment at herself. "I'm not big on keeping it here," she said, "but Rod's got a point. We all have a right to know what the man's got in mind. Better an empty building than a crummy pile of rubble."

"Bless Rod," Heather said under her breath, "That boy has a future. I'll send him to college myself if I have to."

"Did you find out anything last night?"

Heather shook her head. "Just that the bulldozers start this morning."

She spotted Rod and threw her arms around him, almost splashing him with Mr. Maxner's coffee. "Have you thought about calling the television station?"

His eyes widened, and his voice cracked a little with excitement. "Do you think they'd come?"

"Of course they will, if you drop Cole Dennison's name. Run across and use my phone. But hurry. It's almost light."

Her intuition that the workers would be early proved correct; the crane and wrecking ball arrived just after the first tiny sliver of sun peeked over the horizon. The bulldozer operators came next, looking a little surprised at their reception committee and a bit uncertain of what to do about it. Heather suggested they ask their boss, and politely directed them to the nearest pay telephone.

Less than half an hour later the television crew appeared and began setting up a camera and microwave relay dish across the street. The equipment was not yet all in place when the distinctive throb of a helicopter disturbed the quiet morning, and a red-and-silver bird swooped low over the building.

*I might have known,* Heather thought. *Cole Dennison's time is too valuable to travel by mere limousine!*

The helicopter came to rest in the school yard, between the crane and the bulldozers. It whipped up a massive cloud of dust that sent the protesters running for the main steps, where the sheer bulk of the building provided a little protection from the turbulence and the choking cloud.

Heather, who had half expected the dust storm, was already sitting on the top step. She watched Cole Dennison step out of the helicopter, bending to dodge the still-rotating blades, and she felt her insides tighten in anticipation of the coming encounter. It was getting to be a familiar sensation.

He stopped just clear of the rotor blades, and looked over the crowd on the steps. She knew what he was looking for, and she knew the instant he saw her, for he shook his head just a little and started toward the base of the steps. His overcoat was unbuttoned and his hands were deep in his pockets. He did not seem to feel the wind.

Heather was certainly feeling it. Every cell in her body seemed ready to freeze and burst. Her hands were still folded around Mr. Maxner's mug; even though every drop of warmth had been drained from the coffee long ago, the action gave her an illusion of comfort. And it stopped her fingers from trembling, too. She wasn't ashamed to admit it.

There were two men with Cole Dennison; one of them strode up to the base of the steps and folded his arms across his chest. "All right, who's in charge here?" he demanded. "Not that it matters. You're all guilty of criminal trespass, and you'll be arrested if you don't immediately disperse peaceably."

Cole Dennison moved then. "Joe," he recommended, "don't make a bigger fool of yourself than you can help. You're out of your league. Besides, it's not criminal trespass—these are reasonable people. They haven't done an ounce of damage and I'm sure they won't." He climbed the steps slowly as if he were on some sort of royal progress, and the crowd gave way for him. He stopped a bit below Heather and took a relaxed stance with one foot raised a step and his forearm resting on it, as if he was content to stay there for hours. His eyes were on a level with hers. "Right, Miss DeMarco?"

"Good morning, Mr. Dennison," she said calmly. "I'm glad you came out to see your building after all. I'm sorry we all had to go to such trouble to get you here."

He shook his head. "Heather, oh, Heather, a sit-in? You disappoint me. I expected something far more original from you."

A few feet away, Rod cleared his throat and began chanting. "Save our school. Save our school—everybody!"

Cole Dennison turned his head to look incredulously at Rod, and the chant died in midword. "Was this your idea, young man?" he asked mildly.

Rod nodded proudly. "Heather asked me to help, and so I—"

"I might have known. Does every male who associates with you end up doing crazy things, Heather?"

She didn't like the tone of that question. "No one person could have organized this without neighborhood support, Mr. Dennison. You see, Archer's Junction may no longer be an independent town, but it will never let itself deteriorate into just another featureless suburb. This building is a very important part of this community's identity."

There were murmurs of agreement, and Rod started chanting again.

Heather raised her voice. "We fought five years ago to keep the school open—and we lost. But we still have a unique building, and we're not going to let it be destroyed on a tycoon's whim. Look at it, Mr. Dennison. Architects have a word for that—"

He looked up. Directly above his head was a carved stone gargoyle. "And the word is *ghastly,*" he hazarded.

"It's Richardsonian Romanesque," Heather snapped. "With Gothic influences. It's wonderful."

"I don't care what the architectural style is called." He straightened up and addressed the crowd. "I don't think the committee approach is going to work very well here. In fact, I don't intend to discuss the matter any further under these circumstances. There are a couple of options—I can call in the authorities to remove you, since this is private property and you're trespassing on it, or you can name a single representative and we can talk this over somewhere without an audience and see if we can reach some sort of agreement. I'd suggest it be your resident expert here."

There were a few nods.

He looked down at Heather. "How about it? I think we'd get a lot further without the television crew watching."

"I don't know. I kind of like their friendly faces." She tried to unfold her fingers from the mug; they were too stiff to move, but she went on stubbornly, "I'd rather stay right here, Mr. Dennison."

"Heather," he said. "Darling."

He was smiling like a tiger again, she noted. Heather's skin started to crawl in premonition, but it was too late.

His voice sounded soft and confiding, but it carried effortlessly halfway across the school yard. "How did you ever manage to conceive my child when you still insist on calling me 'Mr. Dennison'?"

She winced. There was a ripple of shock through the crowd. "I asked for that," she said, under her breath.

"You certainly did," he said agreeably.

"You aren't using this as a ruse just to get us all away so the wrecking ball can start, are you—Cole, dear?" Her tone was sticky-sweet.

He seemed astounded. "Of course not!"

"Word of honor?"

Cole Dennison grinned. "I'll do better than that. I'll leave a hostage. Joe, I don't believe you've met Miss De-Marco yet, have you? Lucky guy. Joe, sit right here on the top step till I come back to get you. And don't let the bull-dozers drive over you. Now you don't believe I'd risk one of my top executives for this, do you, Heather?" He stretched a hand down to pull her to her feet.

Heather dodged it and pushed herself up from the step. "Yes, but that's beside the point."

Her knees were stiff from the cold, and she stumbled on the way down the hill. Cole's hand, still on her elbow, was the only thing that saved her from a fall. He said amiably, "You're a damn fool, sitting out there in the cold for the sake of an old building. It hasn't got a soul, you know."

"Are you certain of that? You've never even been in-side."

He ignored the interruption. "There must be some-where to get a cup of coffee to warm you up."

Only Cookys, she thought glumly. She knew it was open, for Katherine had stopped at the school this morning to see what all the excitement was about, and then had gone on down to make coffee for the crowd.

But Heather didn't want to take Cole Dennison to Cookys. Even more, she didn't want to let him know that she was an equal partner in the place, and that it was her full-time job.

It wasn't exactly that she wanted to conceal anything from him, she told herself. But surely she wasn't under any moral obligation to correct his mistaken impression, was she? He seemed to have convinced himself that she was a certified, genuine architectural historian, and at the mo-ment, he actually seemed willing to take her seriously. But she could imagine the reaction if she were to tell him that she wasn't an expert on old buildings at all, only on chocolate chips and oatmeal. First he'd laugh, and then he'd go back up the hill and start up one of the bulldozers himself.

"No restaurants," she said firmly. "Though we could certainly use a couple. It's antiques, mostly. We've put a lot of time and energy and money into restoring the turn-of-the-century atmosphere. It's one of the reasons that a shiny new glass building like Dennison Tower wouldn't fit here at all."

Cole frowned. "Funny—I don't recall threatening to build anything like Dennison Tower anywhere in the neighborhood."

They were at the door of Cookys.

"I'll get the coffee," Heather offered, improvising. "But I think we should talk somewhere that we can't be overheard. There's a little courtyard just around the corner—the wind won't be bad there."

Cole shrugged. "You're the one who's freezing, so if you want to sit outside and get colder yet, I'm not going to object. But I'm not letting you out of my sight." He held open the door firmly, and followed her in.

Katherine DeMarco looked relieved. "The coffee's finally done, Heather, but no one has come down to get it."

"Oh, thanks, but we won't need it now. The sit-in seems to be over. Just give us a couple of cups and some double-chocolate-chip, all right?" She groped in her jeans pockets and then gave her mother a crooked smile, hoping she would get the message. "I'll pay you this afternoon."

Katherine's eyes widened. "Heather, what *is* the matter with you? I don't understand you—"

Cole interrupted. "I'm beginning to think nobody does, ma'am. This one's on me, anyway." He passed a ten-dollar bill across the counter and pointed at another tray of cookies. "Throw in a couple of those, too, will you?"

"Oatmeal-raisin?" Heather said hastily. "I was certain you'd be a chocolate type. But those are good. I've tried them before."

Katherine shot one blistering look at Heather as if convinced that she had finally blown a circuit, and then made change in stony silence.

Heather seized the coffee containers and started for the door. "Most men are, you know. Chocolate types."

"And I'm sure you've surveyed a lot of them to find out."

"My share, yes. Why?" Heather smothered a sigh of relief as the door swung shut behind them. She led the way around the Depression glass shop and into the little courtyard, a secluded nook with benches, statues and plants that were just beginning to show the promise of spring. Concrete benches, she thought with a sigh. *Very dumb, Heather, you deserve to freeze your tailbone.*

But the sunshine that was too weak to fight off the breeze was strong enough in this protected little corner to warm the bench. She settled onto it, pulled the lid off her paper cup and took a big swallow. The hot coffee seemed to burn all the way through her body, and she gasped and choked.

Cole grabbed for her tilting cup just before its contents could pour over his knee, and held it till she was breathing normally again. She thought he looked a little hesitant about giving it back at all.

"All right," she said. "Where do we start negotiating?"

"We don't," Cole said calmly. "There's no reason on earth for me to negotiate anything with you."

Heather rummaged in the bag for a cookie. "So the agreement you were referring to is that you get your way and I give in, is that it?"

"It *is* my building, Heather, and it's my right to do anything I want with it. You've got nothing to say about it. I've checked, and it's not even listed on the local register of historic sites." He shook a chiding finger at her. "That was very careless, you know."

Heather took a big bite from her cookie and said agreeably, "Then if we're not negotiating, what are we doing here?"

"We're sitting here and waiting till the excitement dies down up at the school, and the television people go away. I prefer not to have an audience when I get blackmailed into taking action, you see. It's such a bad example for my employees. Then we'll go up there and tour the place."

She chewed thoughtfully, letting the silence draw out. There was a catch here; she was certain of it. "You'll look at it? Really look at it?"

"I plan to study every inch of it," he said grimly. "And you're going to, as well, so that when it's over I won't have any more flak from you about what's done with—"

"Good," Heather interrupted. "That's all I've ever wanted, you know—for you to realize what you're doing, and to really understand what a waste it would be if you actually destroy the school."

It was the first time she had seen him at a loss for words.

"I'm not stupid," she went on blithely. "I certainly know there's no legal way to force you to save that building."

"I thought that was why you were concentrating on the unethical, immoral and illegal ones," he said.

"That hurts my feelings."

"It shouldn't. It's almost a compliment. You have a unique flair for that sort of thing."

She picked the chocolate chips out of her second cookie and stacked them in a neat little pile. "Oh, do you mean last night?" she said airily. "Believe me, that wasn't planned. It just sort of... happened."

"I didn't think you had considered all the possible consequences," he said gravely.

"Like having my fictional pregnancy announced on the television news shows? No, I must admit I didn't anticipate that. I think once you really look at the school, Mr.—" She saw the corner of his mouth twitch and added hastily, "Cole. That painting above the mantel in your office—it's a Monet, isn't it?"

His eyebrows shot up. "What has my taste in art got to do with it?"

"Not only art. Your whole office is a beautiful place. And though I'm no big fan of glass skyscrapers, at least Dennison Tower isn't the worst I've ever seen. You're a lover of beauty, that's obvious, and I don't think you can square it with your conscience to destroy a beautiful building like the school."

"And what if I can? Your definition of beauty and mine may not be the same, Heather."

"Then I lose my bet, don't I? I'm a realist."

His eyes were bright with anticipation. "And you'll actually call off your troops and go away and save someone else's building from demolition? And let me go back to real business, and allow the wrecking crew to work in peace?"

"That's not what you promised," Heather objected. "You said you'd look at it with an open mind—"

"Oh, I'll certainly look at it carefully. But I don't feel very open-minded at the moment. Do you know what it's costing me to keep that crew sitting up there, idle?"

"Not enough to worry you, I bet," she guessed. "So what is it, really, that's bothering you?"

He looked at his wristwatch. "I think we've given the television people enough time to get bored and go away."

*It shouldn't be any concern of mine,* Heather told herself. *But there is something eating at him—and it isn't the cost of delay. It's something much more than that... something he doesn't want to talk about.*

But she put it out of her mind, because right then there were more important things to think about. This was the only chance she would get to change his mind.

"Archer's Junction is a very busy community," she said on the way back up the hill. "Especially on weekends, when antique buffs from all over the state come in to shop. We have some turnover in businesses, of course, but there's practically a waiting list for space. This neighborhood is absolutely unique."

He gave a sort of grunt. "Of course I always enjoy canned chamber of commerce tours, DeMarco, but—"

"If you like," Heather snapped, "I can get you the key to the city, too. But I didn't think you were so shallow that you'd appreciate empty gestures like that."

He laughed. "You're right—it wouldn't sway me. They're such useless things, you see, and I already have a collection from all over the country."

His hand slipped down from her elbow to capture her fingers. Even through the heavy wool of her glove she could feel the electrical jolt of that contact. Did he feel it too? she wondered. He didn't seem to; he apparently wasn't even aware that his grip had shifted.

She said a little breathlessly, "I'm just trying to point out that we could really use more retail space, and there's enough in the school for fifty antique stores. Think about the draw that would be in the winter—shop without ever going outside. Or it could be condos, office space, a day-care center— It could even be a hotel to house all the visitors."

"You're getting wilder by the minute," he said, and stopped at the edge of the school yard to look up at the bulk of the building. "I'm surprised you haven't suggested turning it into a minimum-security prison. It certainly looks like one."

"I've got it," she murmured. "You could make it into a museum filled with your childhood toys and all your memorabilia, and leave it to the city as a monument to our most infamous—I mean famous—citizen. There could even be a whole room devoted to all those keys from all those cities."

"Brat," he said calmly, and let go of her fingers to take the flashlight Joe Hanford held out. He unlocked one of the huge carved front doors and stepped across the threshold. "I'm not being rude," he said over his shoulder. "I'm going first because I'm a gentleman. I wouldn't want you to fall through the weak spots in the floor."

That was almost the last thing he said. It was an odd little procession that trailed through the dark building—Cole, followed by Joe Hanford, followed by Heather.

She wished she could make him see the rooms as she remembered them, when the school had still been in use. They were big rooms, built to hold what had looked like an ever-increasing population of students, with big windows and lots of sunshine and air. Not at all like the new school, she thought, with its climate control and tiny energy-efficient glass panels and brilliant artificial light.

But now the rooms were dark and dirty, and they smelled of mildew and the acrid aftermath of smoke. The fire, so promptly discovered and extinguished, had gutted only a single storeroom in the gymnasium wing, but the smell of it had seeped into the rest of the building. It filled every hallway, every classroom, every closet. Some of the water that had been poured onto the blaze had cascaded down the stairway and through the storeroom floor, and now it stood in puddles in the gymnasium, staining and warping the fine wood. It was no longer the best gym floor in this end of town, and it never could be again.

Cole's nose wrinkled in distaste, but he made no comment, just strode around a puddle and went back into the main part of the building and up the stone stairs, long ago worn smooth by the feet of thousands of young people. But she knew he must be thinking that she was a fool to have underestimated the damage. And she couldn't blame him. It hadn't even occurred to her that the smoke and water from such a small fire could have done so much damage.

But those things, while unsightly and unpleasant, did not affect the strength of the building, she reminded herself.

Whatever Cole Dennison was thinking, however, she had to give him credit for looking carefully. She had half expected that despite his promise to the contrary, this would be a perfunctory tour, just enough for him to be able to argue that of course he had looked at the building. The best she had hoped for was that the school would reach out to him with the same sort of magnetism it had always held for her. But he was really concentrating. In fact, she was a little like a puppy, trailing along at the heels of a master too busy to notice her.

Cole found the tiny winding staircase that led up to the tower, and climbed it eagerly. "Coming, Heather?" he asked, sticking his head back down through the trapdoor at the top.

Heather thought, *Blast him! Of all the moments for him to remember that I'm here, just as he's going up into that open tower!* "No, thanks," she said, and managed to smile. "I'll take your word for the condition of the shingles."

"You're missing a great view. There's even a flagpole on top of the tower."

She clenched her fists till her nails cut into her palms. "I'll take your word for the view, too," she said feebly. "And the flagpole." *If I went up in that tower,* she thought, *they'd have to get the fire department's snorkel truck to rescue me, like a terrified Persian kitten stuck in a tree!*

The stairs creaked, and Cole came back into sight. His hair was windblown and he was grinning, and Heather's hands relaxed and her heart skipped just a little faster. If he was so very pleased with the view . . .

"Definitely a prison," he said. "It's already got the watchtower."

They stopped on the front steps, while Joe Hanford carefully locked the door. Below, in the schoolyard, the helicopter sat silent on its makeshift pad, and the workmen, crammed into the cab of the crane, patiently played cards. Heather took a long breath of fresh air and released it with an unconscious sigh.

"Relieved to get out of there?" Cole asked solicitously.

"Not at all," she flared, and he laughed. "All right," she added, "I admit that concentrated smoke isn't going to catch on as the next hit perfume. But if you ripped off all that plywood and opened the windows, it would soon air out."

He didn't answer.

"So? What do you think?" she prodded.

"It's certainly not what I expected."

Heather nodded. "It's unique. And it's solid, Cole."

He sighed. "That's still a long way from being worth the investment it would take to save it."

She put a small hand on his arm, pleadingly. "Just give it a reprieve for a couple of weeks and think it over. Please?"

"And if I don't? You promised you'd give up the cause, you know. Or are you going to weasel out of that in favor of some more illegal, immoral—"

She shook her head. "Creative—"

"And unethical ways to slow me down?"

She bit her lip and gave an unhappy little sigh. "I can't think of any more," she admitted.

The corner of his mouth twitched. "Oh, I'm sure you will. Joe, tell those guys in the crane that we're not going to knock anything down."

Heather couldn't help it; she uttered a little scream of pure triumphant delight, clutched his arm with both hands and started jumping up and down.

Cole's eyebrows climbed. "For a day or two, at least," he went on. "But don't let them take that equipment away, either." He turned to Heather and put his hands on her shoulders, as if to hold her down to earth. "I'm making no promises about what happens next week. But I will think it over. And after I've had a chance to consider my options—I just might be willing to bargain."

## CHAPTER FOUR

SHE WATCHED the helicopter take off, and shuddered as it dipped and swayed and wobbled and finally disappeared over the treetops. Then she hugged herself a little in delight. She had pulled it off; she was sure of it. If Cole Dennison had still intended to tear down the school, he'd have given the order right then, whether Heather was standing by or not—

*And what makes me so sure?* she asked herself. *Certainly it's not long and intimate knowledge of the man! And he as good as said he knew that I wouldn't quit fighting him. So maybe it's simply strategy—telling me that he'll delay, and then just waiting till my back is turned....*

*No,* she thought. *He doesn't pull his punches like that. I'm sure of it.*

But it was in a much more sober mood that she crossed the street to the brownstone building and took a shower to wipe away the smell of smoke and musty air that clung to her.

What would Cole do? And when would she know?

She saw the young fire captain coming out of the wrought-iron shop just as she was pulling open the front door of Cookys, and waited, half-hoping that he would cross the street and join her. But he only waved and went on. She thought he looked a bit pink with embarrassment.

Gossip must be flying, she thought, after that exchange on the steps of the school. Well, the baby was a good story;

she could hardly blame Archer's Junction for getting all the enjoyment possible out of it. But it was a shame. That was a very nice young man across the street, and now she'd probably never have a chance to know him better.

*Oh, let's feel sorry for ourselves, shall we?* she mocked. *He's certainly not the first man you've ever been attracted to who didn't return the interest, DeMarco. And if he really is interested in you, and is idiot enough not to check out that story about the baby before believing it—well, in that case he's no great loss.*

So the first thing she did, out of sheer perversity, was to get the silly plastic fireman's hat out of the kitchen, put it upside down on the top of the display counter and fill it with samples of their newest recipe, a rich concoction called peanut butter royale.

Katherine watched her silently, with obvious concern. Finally she said, "How did your discussion with Cole Dennison turn out, Heather?"

"Hmm? Oh, everything is going to be fine." She reached for a fresh apron and tucked her hair up under a cap.

"Well, that's certainly a relief," Katherine said dryly. "Do you mind elaborating on what 'everything' includes?"

Heather wasn't listening. "And you have time to make it to your bridge luncheon after all. You don't want to miss that."

"Oh, bridge is nothing compared to the sheer joy this morning has been." Katherine's voice was heavy with irony. "Heather Lynne DeMarco, will you settle down long enough to tell me just why you didn't introduce me to that young man? And why did you let him think I'm the one who owns this place, and you've got nothing to do with it?"

Heather was reaching into the case for a slightly over-browned almond delight. "Well, you see, darling, I just couldn't tell him the truth. If he knew I bake cookies for a living instead of studying old buldings..." She thought it through rapidly, and decided that there was no way her mother would see the humor in the story. "I can't possibly explain, it's far too complicated."

"Make an effort," Katherine said firmly.

Heather straightened abruptly. It was years since Katherine had spoken to her in that tone of voice; before they had gone into partnership together, they had agreed to leave their blood relationship out of the business day. "What's eating you, Mother? You haven't made inquiries about my male friends since I turned twenty-one and moved out on my own!" Then the answer hit her. "Oh...you must have heard about that silly remark of his about the baby."

"No less than a dozen times, in tones that varied from shock to glee. Heather, what in heaven's name—"

"It's nothing, really. There's no baby. And you don't want to hear the whole story, honestly, Mother—"

"Try me!" Katherine ordered.

Heather kissed her mother's cheek. "Go play bridge, darling," she advised. The telephone was ringing, and she grabbed for the excuse. "Cookys. May I help you?"

"I'm trying to reach Heather DeMarco. Can you tell me where I might find her?"

The effect of that slightly husky voice, applied directly to her ear, was astounding; it was like a surge of low-voltage electricity tickling along her nerves. She had been hoping to hear from Cole next week...but to get a call so soon must mean that it was not good news. It hadn't taken him much time to look at his options, she thought with a shiver.

"Speaking," she said weakly.

There was a split-second silence. He sounded surprised. "You?"

"Yes...I sort of work here, sometimes."

"That's the truest thing you've said all day!" Katherine muttered. "That's him, I suppose."

Heather nodded.

"Helping out your mother?" Cole said into her ear.

"How did you know she's my mother?"

"There's rather a strong resemblance. I just realized it, however. I had other things on my mind earlier. Why didn't you introduce me?"

Heather rolled her eyes. "So you could break the news to her about the baby? You'd have enjoyed that, I'm sure—"

Katherine stopped untying her apron strings. "You said there isn't any baby!"

"And furthermore, there never was a baby!" Heather whispered and turned her back on her mother.

"What?" Cole said. "There had better not be any baby."

"Why? Because you've publicly claimed it, so I'd have a wonderful case for getting child support?"

"Never mind. I'll pretend I didn't hear any of that. I was really calling to see if you'd have dinner with me tomorrow. I'm ready to deal."

She swallowed hard. "That didn't take long."

"Time is money. That crane can't sit there forever while I make up my mind, you know."

She caught the telephone between her ear and her shoulder and started rotating cookies in the case. "All right. Dinner."

"Good. I'll pick you up at seven. Wear that slinky little black number again, will you?"

"Can't. Your goons left black-and-blue handprints all over me. Damn," she said as Katherine gave a sharp little scream behind her. "No, Mother, I was not mugged or assaulted or beaten. It was a mistake, all right?"

"How did she ever manage to survive your childhood?" Cole asked curiously. "She must have had a panic attack every time you went out to play."

"Easily. I was a perfectly respectable person till I ran into you. Oh, Cole? One more thing—if you plan to pick me up in the helicopter, forget it."

There was a laughing undercurrent in his voice. "Oh, I won't. It's impossible to sneak out to a lovers' lane in it. But most girls don't think of that right away. I find it fascinating that you did."

*You walked straight into that one, DeMarco,* she told herself. "Need the address?" she asked primly.

"Oh, no. I'll just look for a spot of trouble, and I'm sure you'll be at the center of it. See you tomorrow."

Heather put down the telephone and turned to face her mother with her lower lip caught between her teeth, waiting for the inevitable inquisition. She might be twenty-six years old now, but a mother was a mother forever—whether there was a partnership agreement or not.

Katherine closed her eyes tightly. "You're right," she said through clenched teeth. "I *don't* want to hear the whole story. I'm going to go play bridge instead. That always makes me feel better."

Heather might as well have closed the doors and gone home, for all the good she was at Cookys the rest of the afternoon. She forgot to set the timer and burned Rod's oatmeal-pecan feast, and absentmindedly substituted salt for baking powder and ended up with a hundred of the flattest, most unpleasant-tasting sugar cookies ever to come out of an oven.

The problem was that she couldn't get her mind off Cole Dennison and that unexpected telephone call. Why had he invited her to dinner, anyway? Lunch she could have understood—all the best business deals seemed to be made over lunch—but dinner? And why had he asked her to wear that dress again? He had certainly seemed to enjoy looking at it last night, but surely it was a strange request for a business conference. And what about that reference to lovers' lanes? Was it only to keep her off guard, or had it been almost Freudian—a glimpse into what he was planning?

For there was one possibility that answered all those questions, and more. One particular trade that he might be ready to suggest. A very personal sort of bargain.

No, she told herself uneasily. People didn't make deals like *that,* not in this day and age. It was sexist and discriminatory and—illegal, immoral and unethical, wasn't that what he had called her methods? Did he think, perhaps, that turnabout was only fair? Might he even have concluded that she had asked for something of the sort with that grandstand announcement last night in the hotel ballroom?

*No,* she thought. *He couldn't have made—and kept—all that money if he was in the habit of trading real value for sexual favors, and I doubt he's starting now.*

Nevertheless, once the thought had occurred to her—the possibility that Cole Dennison might offer to save the school if she had an affair with him—it was impossible to put it completely out of her mind again.

SHE THOUGHT ABOUT wearing the oldest and most out-of-fashion garment in her closet, and decided against it only because she concluded that it wouldn't embarrass Cole in the least. Besides, she told herself sternly, there was no sense at all in jumping to conclusions. Perhaps he had offered dinner because it was the only time free in his schedule. Perhaps he had suggested the little black dress because he was taking her to some exclusive night spot. And perhaps he had nothing in mind at all except a flat deal of favor trading, of the sort that could be carried out on any public sidewalk without embarrassment to the passersby.

In any case, she thought, showing a little dignity could not possibly hurt the situation. And it would certainly be a nice change. He probably didn't think she *could* behave like a lady!

So she fought a brief battle with her fiscal conscience at the exclusive clothing boutique down the street from Cookys, and took home a frothy confection in the rich color of an overripe pineapple. It had a heart-shaped neckline, cut fairly low, that slid almost off her shoulders, and long, full sleeves that despite their gauzy sheerness hid the undeniable marks on her upper arms. The skirt drifted down from the narrow waist like a cloud.

The dress made her look like a woodland sprite, Cole told her precisely at seven, when she answered her door. He added that she needed only wings to be angelic. He said it with a perfectly straight face, but she was learning not to trust the twinkle in his eyes, so she thanked him politely and went to get her coat. He handled it as carefully as if it had been Elizabetta Winchester's mink, and Heather had one sharp pang of regret that it wasn't—or something better than an ordinary spring trench coat, at any rate. Then she briskly told herself to be sensible. The dress had been enough of a splurge. She would be months paying for it, and probably would never have occasion to wear it again.

*Still, it was worth it. I can negotiate much better if I feel attractive,* she told herself, *and this dress certainly adds to my self-esteem. Whatever Cole said, he likes the dress—I can see that much in his eyes.*

The car waiting at the curb was a Mercedes stretch limousine, with a uniformed chauffeur standing at attention beside the rear door. "I'm impressed," Heather muttered under her breath as she sank into the dark blue leather seat. "Or did you just borrow it from the hotel?"

"No, it's mine. But I haven't been using it much, and Jason was feeling a little left out of my life. We're using it tonight for his sake," he said earnestly. "I didn't want you to think I brought it just to impress you."

"Oh, I'm sure you didn't—because you can't take it to a lovers' lane either." She bit her tongue, but it was a little too late.

"Well, I never have," he said thoughtfully. "But I'm sure Jason won't mind. He generally brings a book along for when he has to wait for me."

Heather raised her voice. "I didn't mean anything of the—"

"Shall we wait until after dinner, however? I did make reservations, and we're a bit late."

"I'm not interested in lovers' lanes!"

He sounded injured. "Well, *I'm* certainly not the one who brought up the subject."

*So much for dignity,* Heather told herself. *There is something about this man that makes you self-destruct, DeMarco. When are you going to learn?*

The limousine swept to a halt in front of the Palace Grande Hotel, and the doorman sprang to attention and rushed over to greet them. Cole helped her out as carefully as if she were a piece of delicate crystal. Inside, he snapped his fingers for a bellman and sent her coat off to the checkroom—one more difference between mink and ordinary waterproof poplin, Heather told herself—and said, as he guided her across the glittering two-story lobby, "I think you'll enjoy this. The new chef has a very light hand with sauces, and his desserts . . ."

Heather wasn't listening. She was eyeing the waiting elevator with trepidation. Cole was taking her to the rooftop restaurant.

*It's all right,* she told herself, and clutched at a brass railing in the little Art Deco elevator. *The building really isn't all that tall. Remember to breathe deeply and evenly, and choose your seat carefully, so you can't see out the window. . . .*

But there wasn't time enough to plan it out, to think it through, to prepare herself. The doors closed and the elevator exploded upward with a silent swoosh, bursting up through the glass ceiling of the lobby and out into the night—

*Out!* she thought, in black panic.

"Isn't it a gorgeous view?" Cole murmured.

Heather gave a strangled little scream as the elevator wall that she had thought was a smoked mirror became a clear window looking out over the city, and the world fell away beneath her toes at a terrifying pace.

She was squeezing the brass railing till her hands ached. "Heights," she managed to whimper. "I'm afraid of heights. . . ."

He looked stunned. "What do you mean? You were in my office the other day—"

"I rehearsed it. And I couldn't see out then. Not like this." Her eyes were tightly closed, but it was too late; the brief, inescapable glimpse she had gotten had been too much.

"Oh, good God." His arms were around her, tightly. "We have to go up, Heather. The damned elevator only has two stops. Don't look."

"I'm not looking," she gasped. "But it doesn't help, because I can't stop thinking—"

His mouth came down on hers almost harshly, with a kind of desperate determination. Heather's eyes snapped open in astonishment at the sudden assault. Didn't the man have any sensitivity at all? Here she was, in mental agony, and all he saw was an opportunity to snatch a kiss! He deserved to be kicked—

But then his lips softened and began to caress hers, and the same aching paralysis that had held her captive the first time he kissed her crept over her again. By the time the elevator slid to a smooth stop on the top floor of the hotel, she was no longer thinking about kicking him. She was standing on her toes, her body taut against him, her fingers curled into the hair at the nape of his neck. It was a full five seconds after the elevator had stopped before she realized that the doors had opened, and then it only crossed her mind because he stopped kissing her.

"What was that all about?" Heather asked hazily.

"It was the only way I could think of to take your mind off it." He was still holding her, as if he thought that she'd collapse if he let her go.

"Off—oh. That."

A blond woman in flame-red gauze who was waiting outside the elevator said snidely, "I'd say you obviously succeeded, Cole, dear. Now do you suppose the rest of us could use the elevator?"

Heather's head snapped around. There was only a small knot of people—half a dozen, perhaps—waiting in the tiny lobby, but to her guilty eyes it looked like a hundred accusing faces were waiting for an explanation of this ridiculous scene. And the blonde was one of the women who had been in that group at the cocktail party—the group

Heather had used as cover. "I was just feeling a little queasy, you see," she began uncertainly, "and—"

The blonde's eyes dropped meaningfully to Heather's waistline, where Cole's hands were still resting.

The flood of embarrassment started in Heather's toes and scorched its way upward, burning like red-hot lava.

*Don't let it get to you,* she told herself desperately. *So what if she heard your crazy announcement? Lots of people did.*

And that thought didn't help at all.

Cole was smiling, but there was no humor in it. "Nothing much to see yet, is there, Ashley?" he said coolly. "It takes a little time, I'm afraid." He almost lifted Heather off the elevator.

When she got her voice back, she snapped, "Must you go around acting like a proud papa?"

He shrugged. "What was I supposed to do? Just stand by and let you have hysterics? And once Ashley had seen me kissing you, it was a little late for explanations. Be realistic, Heather. That kind of female shark is only happy if she has fresh news to pass along."

"Well, that tidbit would be getting stale by now if you'd leave it alone."

"Feeling better?"

"A little, thank you." The fact that her feet were on something solid steadied her enough that she could take a deep breath and look cautiously around the little foyer and into the adjoining restaurant. The sight was not reassuring. The walls were mostly glass, and every table was carefully placed to take advantage of what most people would call a wonderful view.

Cole was watching her. "Very little, I'd say."

He summoned a busboy who was hovering nearby with his mouth hanging open in surprise. "Make yourself useful, would you, and get the lady a brandy?"

"I don't want a brandy," Heather countered. "I want to get back down below the tenth floor. Just show me to the stairs."

"There's an inside elevator. Unless that's a problem, too."

"No, I'm all right in ordinary elevators, as long as I don't get surprised."

"And it doesn't bother you below the tenth floor?"

"Usually not, unless it's a balcony or something. But the worst of it is, it's not predictable. And if I don't have a chance to prepare myself..." *You're babbling,* she told herself, but she couldn't seem to stop. "I know it's dumb—"

He shook his head. "Unusual. Not dumb."

"Well, embarrassing, then. There's no sensible explanation for it. I mean, it's not like I fell off a cliff when I was a child, or was in a skyscraper during an earthquake, or anything that would have given me a reason for being afraid."

The busboy was still hovering in the doorway, apparently uncertain of whose orders to follow. Cole called him back. "Skip the brandy, and ask the chef to send down some of that Alaskan king salmon and the trimmings for us."

"Down? Where are we going?" Heather asked warily.

"Below the tenth floor." It was brusque, and the hand on her arm did not invite further discussion, so she didn't argue. Besides, anything would be better than confronting that wall of glass for another minute.

But when the elevator stopped at six and the doors opened on what was obviously a quiet floor of guest rooms, not the lobby she had expected, Heather turned to Cole in surprise.

"My suite," he said. "This is probably better, anyway. It's more private for our discussion."

*Don't get paranoid,* Heather told herself. *If it was something he couldn't discuss in public, he never would have taken you to the rooftop in the first place.*

But there was a tremor deep inside her that was almost worse than her fear of heights had ever been.

The suite surprised her; it was more like an apartment in size. It was beautifully decorated in perfectly harmonizing colors, with lush carpets and furniture and draperies and all the correct accessories, but it left her feeling cold. There was not a personal touch to be seen anywhere—not so much as a book, a candy wrapper or a framed photograph to let her know it was his. If he hadn't pulled the key from his pocket, she'd have sworn it was simply an anonymous hotel room like any other.

*And perhaps that's exactly what it is,* said a nagging little suspicion that could not be squelched. *An ordinary hotel suite acquired just for the occasion. Perhaps he intended all along that we'd end up here.*

"Not what you expected?" he said easily. "My house was supposed to be completed by now, so I didn't mind being agreeable when the people who bought my apartment wanted immediate possession. This is only a stopgap."

The knot in Heather's chest loosened a little.

"But I should have known better than to believe that things would stay on schedule."

His tone was cynical, and it almost seemed to be directed at Heather. She wondered why.

"Now how about that glass of brandy?"

"Not on an empty stomach, thanks." She was looking around cautiously. Heavy draperies were drawn tightly on the windows—almost all the windows, she corrected; half the wall space was taken up by them, and there was one that hadn't been covered. The glimpse of the city skyline it provided was as hypnotically tantalizing as the gaze of a snake, she thought. She couldn't seem to take her eyes off it.

Cole saw where she was looking, and crossed the room quickly to close the draperies. "Can't they do something about phobias like that?" he asked.

"Oh, yes." She gave a sigh of relief when the view disappeared, and sat down in a wing-backed chair. Her knees weren't quite steady yet. "You should have seen me a year or two ago, before I took the desensitizing class and learned to cope with it."

"This is coping? I think I'd ask for my money back." There was a wet bar concealed in a bank of cabinets along the living room wall; he began inspecting its contents. "How about sherry?"

"That's fine. Perhaps we should get our little discussion out of the way?"

He shrugged. "It's all right with me."

But he didn't seem inclined to proceed. Finally, Heather said, "I presume you mean that you've got some possible plans for the school, and you want to see which one I like best before you proceed."

He turned around at that, in blank astonishment. "*I want to see which one you like best?* You are one gigantic bundle of nerve, Heather DeMarco! Trying to save that damned school has been the biggest aggravation of my life, and don't tell me again how good I'll feel about myself when it's finished. If I want to feel good, I'll go play a couple of sets of tennis, or lie in the sun in the Caribbean for a few days. Or run the wrecking ball myself—now *that* would make me feel good!"

Heather didn't move. "If you weren't willing to negotiate that, I wouldn't be here, would I?"

"No. You're right. I'm ready to do some dealing." He brought her a stemmed crystal sherry glass and perched on the arm of the matching chair with a Scotch and soda in his hand. "I'm just pointing out that there is no reason on earth I should cut you any slack, DeMarco. You got me into this mess and you are damned well going to get me out."

"Which mess are we talking about? If it's the fact that your society friends still seem to think I'm pregnant, you've got no one to blame but yourself."

He shook his head. "It's not that. As far as I'm concerned, people like Ashley can think what they like. They generally do, anyway. The truth doesn't faze them."

"Then what mess are we talking about?"

He pushed an ice cube around in his Scotch and soda with his index finger. "It's my house. It's already behind schedule, and now you have single-handedly put a stop to the whole project."

Now she was thoroughly confused, and also half-convinced that he'd lost his mind. "I swear I don't know anything about any house, Cole."

"Ignorance is no excuse." He set the drink aside. "If you're going to go around bursting into people's lives like a chain-saw-wielding maniac, you're responsible for the consequences. All of the consequences."

"I don't see—"

"I'm not surprised, so I'll start at the beginning. You see, Heather, that event last Thursday night was supposed to be an engagement party. It was *my* engagement party—until, of course, you made your grandstand announcement."

It hit her with the weight of a hammer, and her heart seemed to cascade toward her toes under the force. She couldn't decide whether to cry and throw herself on his mercy, or give way to the hysterical giggles that she couldn't quite swallow.

*And you thought when you came in here that he might have illicit designs on you, DeMarco,* she told herself. *What an idiot you are!*

## CHAPTER FIVE

SHE SWALLOWED her sherry a little too fast, and her voice was rough around the edges as she said, "So what does your messed-up engagement party have to do with your house?"

"How gracious of you to apologize," Cole murmured. "I'm touched by the depth of your regret. Your overwhelming remorse actually brings a tear to my sensitive eye—"

"So I'm sorry, already," Heather snapped. "But if you're going to suggest that I go have a chat with your erstwhile fiancée and explain it all, no thanks. If she doesn't trust you any more than to call off the engagement because of that one little incident, she isn't going to believe me, either."

*"One little incident?"*

The tone of his voice annoyed her unreasonably, and she glanced up at him through her lashes and struck back. "A tiny thing like one illegitimate baby," she mused, "and she let it come between her and all your lovely money? *I'd* certainly never be so shortsighted." She frowned thoughtfully at her sherry glass. "Unless, of course, it wasn't the first time."

The noise he uttered made Heather glad that his hands were on his glass and not on her throat.

But the perverse imp that had grabbed control of her tongue just kept on going. "Or perhaps she knows that you're in the habit of kissing every female who comes into your office. In that case, I can see why she might have doubts—"

"You'll notice," he said grimly, "that I haven't asked you to speak to her. Your idea of straightening things out, Heather, could do nothing but make them worse."

"That's what I just said—at least, I think it is. Though I assure you I am generally very respectable and ordinary and trustworthy, except where I'm associated with you." She smiled at him. "I think I'm allergic to you, Cole."

He growled something, but a rap on the door drowned out the words. Heather thought it was just as well she hadn't heard him clearly.

Cole opened the door, and a waiter and two busboys wheeled in a huge silver cart, parked it next to the round table, removed the enormous dome that covered it and went silently to work laying two places and serving up the first course. Wonderful aromas began drifting up from the serving dishes, reminding Heather that Cookys had been so busy today that she hadn't bothered with lunch.

Cole watched till the wine was opened and the last spoon was set in place before he moved from his perch on the arm of the chair. "We'll take care of serving the rest ourselves," he said, "and call you to collect the wreckage." He ushered them out and came back to seat Heather at the table.

She had spent the time thinking about the scene that must have followed her exit from the cocktail party. Had his fiancée pitched an hysterical fit in front of everyone? Had she waited, perhaps, until the champagne toast was proposed in their honor, and then denied the announcement? Or had they argued it out in whispers, behind shielding hands and painted-on smiles? That seemed far more likely, Heather thought with regret. How very dull!

"The fiancée," she said suddenly. "She's the female who was wearing gold tissue that night, of course. I thought she was married. The guard called her Mrs. Something—now what was it?"

He looked a bit wary. "I don't see why you need to know."

"She looked like a circus horse with that headdress on," Heather mused. "Oh, I've got it now. Elizabetta Winchester. Of course, she's Jack Winchester's widow. That explains the headdress, too. Wasn't she an exotic dancer before he married her?"

"She was a fashion model," Cole said crisply.

Heather shrugged. "Sorry. Well, that explains why she wasn't worried about giving up all your lovely money. Jack Winchester must have left her bags of the stuff. Don't you have enough cash of your own, Cole? Do you have to marry more? Oh—I beg your pardon. I forgot for an instant that it was all off." She watched him warily for a moment, and decided it would be prudent to change the subject. "So what has all this got to do with your house?"

He filled her wineglass. "The house was to be a wedding gift to Elizabetta, and she was to have a free hand in finishing and decorating it. It was all supposed to be done by now. But Elizabetta's mother has been ill, and Elizabetta—"

She couldn't help it. "Don't you ever call her Liz or something? I can't quite picture this at the breakfast table, you know. 'Elizabetta, darling, would you pass me the toast, please?' or 'I'll be late home from the office tonight, Elizabetta, dearest—' "

He leaned back in his chair and looked her over. "If you don't mind, Heather."

"Very well," she said hastily. "Carry on." She picked up her spoon again.

"Elizabetta has been in the South of France with her mother for three months, and the house has been at a dead standstill."

"I'm very sorry, but you can hardly blame me for that, can you?"

"Not precisely, I suppose. But I can't move into an unfinished shell of a house, can I? And now that the engagement is at an end, Elizabetta is scarcely going to be finishing it up, is she?"

"I don't know," Heather said, with honest interest. "Have you asked her?"

"She left the city yesterday morning," he said coldly.

*So that's why you made up your mind so quickly,* Heather thought. *As soon as you heard about her departure...* "Not a trip she had planned to take, I gather?" she asked solicitously.

"The story is that she went to visit her grandmother, who has not been in good health."

Heather frowned. "I think I'd have second thoughts if I were you," she mused. "All these sick women in the family—she'll probably end up as some kind of invalid herself." He began to growl, and she went on smoothly, "You're not seriously going to hold all this against me, are you, Cole? I mean, it would be awfully petty of you to tear down the school just because you're mad at me."

"Ah, yes, the school." At that moment, he looked more like a tiger than ever before, and Heather was sorry she had reminded him. "I propose that we make a trade," he said crisply. "You take care of supervising the finishing details so I can move into my house, and I—"

Heather shook her head in disbelief. "Me? Why don't you hire a decorator?"

"And end up with something that looks like this?" He looked around the suite with a shrug. "Besides, it's not exactly to the wallpaper stage yet—and it won't be for a while. I'm talking about things like what sort of heat lamps to use in the bathrooms and whether the closet doors should have mirrors and how deep the carved relief should be on the drawing room mantel. The kinds of pesky details that drive me crazy."

"And of course you don't care if I go crazy."

A smile tugged at the corner of his mouth. "That might be an added benefit."

"Cole, even your secretary must know a whole lot more than I do about what you like—"

"My secretary," he said blandly, "is too busy even to keep unauthorized people out of my office. I couldn't possibly add my house to her burdens." He removed her empty soup plate and found the plates of king salmon and tiny perfect vegetables on the cart.

"All right. Some of your society friends, then."

"They all seem to have sided with Elizabetta."

"How ignoble of them," she sympathized.

"Besides, I'd like to have it done soon—like before summer arrives. Any one of them would play with it for a year, triple the expenses and then want to have a tea for her favorite charity before I could move in. No, Heather, let's face it—you're the best choice I've got. You're the expert, after all."

She had completely forgotten that she was supposed to be an expert. She gave a painful little whimper. "Cole, I don't think—"

He didn't look up from his plate. "If I have to spend all my time on the house," he pointed out calmly, "I simply won't have the necessary hours to work with the architects on the school, to see what they might have come up with." It was very soft. "It would be such a pity if all your effort came to nothing."

"That's not negotiation," she objected. "It's blackmail."

He shook his head. "No, it's emotional pressure. If I told you I'd tear the school down if you didn't volunteer your time to my house, *that* would be blackmail." He smiled across at her and refilled her wineglass.

"Well, that's what you mean, isn't it?" She sighed. "I don't suppose I have a choice."

"Of course you do. But I'm glad you're choosing wisely. By the way, in case you're thinking of turning my house into a bordello—"

"That had not occurred to me."

"It would have, sooner or later," he said comfortably. "Let me make it plain that I'm not handing it over to you without restraint. I expect to have approval of everything you do. You choose what you think is best, and I'll tell you if I disagree. Just don't bring me a hundred samples, or we'll be right back where we started."

She clicked her heels together under the table and saluted. "Sir, I can't wait to begin, sir. It's going to be such a fun job, sir."

"Every good negotiation should end with a little pain on both sides. Besides, it will broaden your experience if you give up old buildings for a while. You might learn to like new ones. And," he added thoughtfully, "it will keep you out of my hair."

She stared at him for half a minute while thinking, and then put down her fork. "You're right," she said finally. "About how there should be a little pain on both sides, I mean. And I think you're dodging yours." She held up a warning hand at his protest. "Don't expect me to be sympathetic because you've lost Elizabetta. Why should I care? I'm talking about the school. I haven't heard any definite plans for what you're going to do with it."

"Dammit, Heather, I can't tell you what I'll do with it, because I don't know."

She placed her elbows firmly on the edge of the table and stared at him. "You will guarantee that the building stands, and is put to a useful purpose, or I don't deal. Otherwise you're getting everything you want, and when your house is done all you have to do is tell me how sorry you are that an alternative use for the school just didn't work out—and send the bulldozers in."

"Do you think I'd do that?" He sounded as if she had wounded him severely.

*No,* she thought. *I don't. Left to myself, I'd trust your gentlemanly instincts, like the fool I am!* But of course she wasn't about to tell him that. "I'm certainly not dumb enough to walk into it blindly, Cole." She speared the last bite of salmon on her plate.

"All right. You've got my word of honor."

"Thank you. I'd like it notarized," she said calmly.

"Dammit, Heather—"

"And then I'll take a look at your house, and I'll let you know if we've got a deal."

"Now, wait a minute—"

"You got to look at the school before you took on the challenge," she reminded.

He sighed. "All right. Tomorrow?"

"Morning. I have to work in the afternoon." She thoughtfully savored the last snow pea pod, and said suddenly, "You're doing this to get even with her, aren't you?"

His eyebrows climbed. "With Elizabetta? Nonsense."

"Of course you are. She rejected you in public, and you want to show her how silly she's being. But it's going to backfire on you. Having me involved with the house is just going to make the scandal and the talk worse, and make it even longer before she cools off enough to forgive you.

You'd be a lot better off to go talk to Elizabetta honestly and tell her what happened."

"Thank you for your advice, Heather. I'm sure you'll pardon me for not chasing halfway across the country to act on it." He pushed back his chair and began inspecting the lower level of the cart, looking for dessert.

"So you do know where she is," she said shrewdly. "You know, it wouldn't hurt you to plead, Cole. You have to admit the woman got a shock."

"It's not likely to be the last time."

"Well, I like that! I certainly don't plan to crash any more parties. Oh, I see. You didn't mean just me. In your position, you're apt to be accused of all sorts of things, true or not."

"Mostly not," he agreed. "But occasionally true." He found the crème caramel and put a serving in front of her.

Heather played with the syrupy sauce. "And you're not going to set any precedents, is that it? It's Elizabetta who will have to give in?"

"I don't recall asking you to counsel me on how to deal with Elizabetta," he said calmly. "What do you think makes you an expert, anyway? I don't see any evidence of a great love in your life."

"I've had my share of masculine interest," Heather said stiffly. "And how would you know whether there's a special man in my life, anyway?"

"Because no one fainted—or threatened to punch me, either—at the school yesterday when I brought up the subject of our baby."

She pushed away her plate and folded her arms across her chest. "Maybe the man in my life just didn't happen to be there."

He shrugged that off without comment and came around the table to hold her chair. "If you're finished playing with that caramel sauce..."

The lack of reaction infuriated her. For all he knew, there were a dozen special men in her life, and he had no right to act as if she couldn't possibly attract even one! "You've made some rather large assumptions, you know, Cole. And it sounds to me as if Elizabetta has, too."

He looked vaguely interested. "What sort of assumptions?"

"I never once said it was *your* baby, you know—just mine." She stood up, and her shoulder brushed against his chest. Somehow, silently, in that half-second space of time, he had moved, and now she found herself entangled in a triangle formed by the chair, the table and him.

"But darling, I would never insult a lady's honor by questioning it." It was a sultry murmur, so close that it stirred her hair. "Even if I don't seem to recall the precise circumstances."

His left arm closed very gently around her, and his other hand came up to nudge her chin. The two inches of air that was left between them seemed to crackle with a supercharged current; it certainly didn't have any breathable oxygen left in it, and Heather's lungs were aching from the lack. It was almost a relief when he eased across the last half step that separated them, for then the electrical field seemed to ground itself. Instead of stinging them, or holding them off from each other any longer, it surrounded them instead with a protective net, keeping them safe from anything that might seek to interfere.

The kiss in the elevator, like the one that first day in his office, had taken her by surprise. But this time he seemed to be in no hurry. It was probably only a matter of seconds that they stood there, his hand cupping her face, Heather's eyes dilating to great brown pools as she stared up at him, but it seemed like aeons. This time she knew what to expect—she knew what effect his kiss would have on her—and she knew, too, that she should stop this now, before it could go any further. But her vocal cords seemed to have gone off on vacation, and all she could do was make a little whimpering sound that could just as easily have been begging as demurring.

And so when he bent his head to take her mouth it was like nothing she had ever experienced before, for this kiss was neither curious nor desperate, as its predecessors had been. Instead, it was full of certainty and knowledge, and the effect was even more devastating. She could not even breathe or move—she could do no more than cling to him.

"And a pity it is that I don't remember, too," he murmured. His voice was a little unsteady.

Something in Heather's brain seemed to snap back into place. "All right," she said breathlessly. "You've made your point. You've got no qualms and no conscience, so I can't possibly stay ahead of you, and I've finally learned better than to try."

He was still holding her intimately close. His lips trailed softly from her temple down over her cheek until his tongue darted against the corner of her mouth. "You wouldn't like to remind me?" he suggested hopefully. "Of what it's like for us to be lovers, I mean. I'd try my best to be a good student."

If merely kissing him was such a shattering experience, then making love with him would be terrifying, Heather thought.

"I'm sure you would. I mean—" She saw the gleam of humor spring into his eyes, and she stumbled over her words. "No. I'm not interested in going to bed with you. And I'd appreciate it if you didn't kiss me again." She managed to get both her hands against his chest, and pushed.

She might as well have been shoving a brick wall. "Why?" he countered lazily. "You're not allergic to me after all. At least, you're not breaking out in any spots that I can see. I'd be happy to inspect the rest of you—"

She pushed a little harder, and his grip loosened. "I don't kiss men who are engaged to other women," she snapped.

Cole looked innocently astonished. "But I'm not, Heather, darling. Remember? You took good care of that. Shall we sit down and talk about it?"

He drew her toward the sitting area, and his hand, firmly clasped on her elbow, prevented her from taking the wing-backed chair she had occupied earlier, and guided her toward the couch instead. Heather's knees were trembling; she told herself that was the only reason she didn't stay stubbornly on her feet.

He sat down beside her. Somewhat to her surprise, though he put his arm across the back of the couch, he did not touch her. He just leaned back into the deep cushions, perfectly at ease, and smiled at her.

The tiger's smile again, she thought. "I suppose you think this is all part of the deal for the school, too."

His fingertips caressed a lock of her hair, disarranged by their embrace. She had never known before that mere strands of hair could pass along a sensation, as sensitively as any nerve. "Well, we haven't exactly concluded the details yet, have we?"

"We certainly have—the house for the school. And that's all."

There was a twinkle in his eyes. "If you insist," he said agreeably. "But I thought you didn't want to commit yourself to an agreement until you'd seen the house."

She gulped. *Trust you to make a fool of yourself, De-Marco,* she thought bitterly. She licked her lips nervously and stole a glance at Cole from the corner of her eye. He was watching her as if he was fascinated—or repulsed.

"Why don't you tell me about it?" she managed finally. "The house, I mean." She sounded a little desperate, and she knew it.

He shrugged. "I'd much rather let you form your own impressions tomorrow, without any prior prejudices." His fingertips moved through the curtain of hair and began to make small circles on the nape of her neck.

*That certainly got me nowhere,* Heather thought. "Then let's talk about the school," she said firmly. "Now that you've decided to actually do it—"

"Pending your agreement to take care of the house," he murmured. "And any further negotiations that might come up."

Heather tried to ignore that. "You must have some ideas for it already. I certainly do."

"You have such a busy little mind, Heather."

"I think apartments would be best. Most of those rooms have sixteen-foot ceilings."

"And a leaky roof."

"They'd make lovely studio apartments. You could build in a balcony halfway up to make space for a bedroom, and—" She slid abruptly to the edge of the couch, feeling that if he continued to draw those slow, sensual circles at the nape of her neck for one more minute she would probably go mad. "Do you have some paper? I'll show you."

"Somewhere, I suppose." He did not sound inclined to seek it out.

"Well, I've got some in my handbag." She jumped up and crossed the room.

"As long as you're up, I think we overlooked the coffee. I'd certainly like a cup." He added something under his breath. Heather thought it sounded like, "Since I'm not likely to be getting anything else."

*At least he's finally gotten the message,* she thought. "Let's see—I didn't notice yesterday. Do you take cream and sugar?"

"No. I prefer my coffee—like the rest of my vices—to be straightforward."

She decided it would be prudent to ignore that one altogether, and stayed cautiously on the opposite side of the low table when she brought his cup. Then she took the wing chair instead of sitting down beside him once more.

He did not comment, but it was plain from the glimmer in his eyes that she wasn't fooling anyone by running away.

Heather flipped open a small notebook and started to draw. "Like this," she said. "I'm sure I don't have the dimensions right, but this is the old science lab. It's huge, and there could be two bedrooms and a bath upstairs..."

He wasn't looking at the page, but at her. "Just what is your fascination with the school?" he asked finally. "It's got to be more than just the building—there are hundreds of old buildings. And you couldn't know which room was which, from that tour in the dark yesterday. I certainly didn't see any science lab."

"You could call it old school ties. My father taught chemistry in that old lab for years."

"Did he move on to the new school?"

"No. He died before it was finished." She didn't stop sketching. "In the smaller classrooms, you could have a single bedroom upstairs. That wouldn't even take a wall, just a railing of some sort, because you wouldn't need the same sort of privacy with only one—"

"I'll take your word for that," he murmured. "I like privacy, myself."

Heather could feel herself turning pink.

"Obviously you won't be renting one of those apartments," he went on smoothly. "Because of the open railing and all. I'll keep that in mind when I think about occupancy rates." He finished his coffee, put the cup and saucer aside and came to sit on the arm of her chair. "So I can look more closely at your drawings," he said smoothly.

It was worse than sitting beside him on the couch; here he was slightly above her, and every breath he took stirred her hair and tickled straight through her scalp and into her brain. And there was not a single thing she could say about it; she had invited it herself. So she swallowed hard and kept on talking about efficient kitchenettes tucked into corners beneath balconies, and spiral wrought-iron staircases, and he listened without comment until she almost began to believe that he was as intent on her drawings as she was trying to be. "On the top floor you could do the same thing, except in the wings where the ceilings are lower," she began. "And think of the lovely little nooks and corners those rooms have—far more attractive than modern boxes, don't you think?"

Then she made the mistake of looking up at him, and she knew that he had been simply biding his time, and that he hadn't given up the game at all. "Heather," he said briefly, very softly. "Damn the school."

She clutched her pencil as if it were a life belt, so tightly that her wrist ached. His hand came to rest on the side of her throat, his fingertips pressed lightly against the pulse point, and a moment later, as if that contact had answered a question to his satisfaction, he leaned toward her.

Just as his mouth brushed hers, she heard something—the lock clicking, perhaps—and she tried to pull away. But

Cole wouldn't let her go, and so she didn't see the man who stood in the doorway; she only heard him say quietly, "Excuse me, sir. I didn't mean to intrude."

Cole sighed. "That's why I want my house finished," he muttered. "At least the damn thing's got a back door."

Heather tried to disappear into the depths of the chair. Not that the man in the doorway was paying any attention to her at all. The well-trained servant, she thought, no doubt experienced at discreetly ignoring a woman's presence—and probably even her slightly disheveled appearance. He certainly didn't have a hair out of place himself; he looked like a caricature of a gentleman's gentleman.

Cole stood up. "It's not your fault, Stanley. I didn't expect you to come up the fire escape, that's sure. Would you call down and have Jason bring the car around?"

Heather gladly gathered up her handbag. "Would you like me to leave my sketches?" she asked. She was trying for flippancy, but something had happened to her voice along the way and it came out low and rather husky.

"Why not? I'll need something to put me to sleep."

Before she could quite decide if she'd been insulted, she was downstairs, being tucked into the limousine. It surprised her a little that he had called for the car, for surely it would have been more like him to dismiss the chauffeur rather than have yet another audience. Unless, of course, he intended to send her home alone. She didn't quite know if she should be glad at that possibility, or resentful. At least it would avoid the question of lovers' lanes....

But the Mercedes swept straight across the city to Archer's Junction, and Cole behaved himself like a perfect gentleman, right up to the moment at the door of her apartment when he took her key out of the lock, put it back into her hand and said, "Aren't you going to invite me in for coffee?"

"What kind of a fool do you think I am? Besides, you've had coffee. And I don't want to keep Jason up too late."

"His mother will appreciate your thoughtfulness. A good-night kiss, then?"

"I think you've already had that, too."

But he didn't seem to be listening—at least he'd already put his arms around her—and there really was no way to stop him short of waking her neighbors. So she dutifully turned her face up to his and waited.

Nothing. After a few seconds she opened one eye a fraction.

"Since I'm coming back in just a few hours to take you on a house tour—" he began.

"Whatever you've got in mind, Cole, the answer is no."

A delighted grin spread across his face, lighting every feature. "Let me see. In that case, the question is, you don't mind if I stay overnight, do you?"

She gasped.

"That way I can collect a good-morning kiss, too—Ouch! That was a perfectly good ankle till you kicked it. You might not be carrying a gun, DeMarco, but you're certainly armed and dangerous."

"You asked for it."

"And so have you," he muttered. He swept her back over his arm in a Hollywood sort of embrace, and if she had struggled she'd have ended up in an ignominious heap on the floor. So she didn't bother to struggle.

It was a long and sultry kiss that seemed to drag sensations all the way from her toes, and it left her wondering if the flippant comment she had made over dinner—about being allergic to him—might actually be true after all.

For while she wasn't breaking out in spots and rashes, every cell inside her was shivering and shaking, itchy and sensitive to the touch—exactly as if she had contracted the world's worse case of hives.

# CHAPTER SIX

AND YOU WOULD HAVE *taken his word,* she jeered at herself. *His word of honor as a gentleman. The truth is, you simply cannot trust a man like that one.*

He kissed her the very first time she met him, Heather reminded herself, without any concern about whether she was willing to be kissed. And he didn't have the tidy excuse of a broken engagement to cover that episode! It didn't matter a damn to him that day that he had a fiancée waiting in the wings. And it wouldn't have bothered him tonight, either. He saw something he wanted, and he went after it.

Did he do that sort of thing often? Was that why Elizabetta had been so unforgiving about the embarrassing scene at her engagement party? It had, after all, been only a minor misunderstanding—unless something else lay beneath it. Something that Heather didn't know.

Even someone as uninterested in social gossip as Heather was couldn't avoid knowing there had been no lack of feminine names connected with Cole Dennison's over the years. Did he expect that kind of freedom to continue after he was married? Was he so certain that Elizabetta would eventually give in, that she would put up with any amount of scandal and gossip in order to have him, that he did not feel it necessary to bend? He certainly possessed that kind of ego, she thought. There were half a dozen examples of it—the primary one being that sizzling kiss in his office.

And now she had another illustration, for there was certainly no reason for him to involve Heather in the work on his house, unless—as she had suspected from the beginning—it was no more than a scheme to get Elizabetta's attention.

Perhaps, she thought, Elizabetta wasn't so foolish after all, in breaking her engagement and leaving town. Perhaps she had left because she didn't trust herself to hold out against Cole's charm. The man could melt resistance like a propane torch melted butter.

And the only sensible course for someone in Heather's position was to stay as far away from him as possible.

*And just how do you propose to do that?* she asked herself. *Call him up right now and tell him not to come tomorrow, because you don't want to see his house and the deal is off? Or I suppose you could put a quarantine sign on your door in the morning—but then he'd only smile and say that he was willing to risk exposure! And in either case, the school would be the forfeit.*

He wouldn't destroy it cold-bloodedly, simply because she had refused to deal; she was fairly certain of that. But the fact was, it didn't matter to him whether the school stood or not. And in the end, she thought, it made no difference whether he destroyed it out of revenge or out of apathy. The school would still be gone, no matter what his motives.

She growled a little—how did she manage to get herself into these predicaments?—and went to change the pineapple-colored dress for jeans and an old college sweatshirt. If she was going to play the expert tomorrow when she saw Cole's house, she'd better do a little research tonight.

The supermarket in the next suburb was open all night, but only a few diehard patrons were in the aisles. There was a harried young father with a screaming baby in the diaper aisle, and a couple of kids who looked too young to legally purchase the beer they were carrying. Heather got a cup of coffee at the deli counter and went straight to the magazine section.

There were dozens of publications that promised to give her insight into how to design, decorate and finish her home. There were magazines that specialized in traditional houses, in Victorians, in contemporaries, in Colonials. There were special magazines on kitchens, on bathrooms, on entertainment centers—even one that covered only floor tiles, for heaven's sake.

"It would help a whole lot if he'd at least told me what sort of house it is," she muttered as she staggered toward the front of the store with a pile of more than two dozen magazines. They made a sad hole in her budget.

"I wonder what he'd say if I submitted an expense account," she mused on her way home. "Even an expert needs tools to work with, after all."

But when the doorbell rang promptly at nine the next morning, Heather hastily shoved the magazines under the edge of the couch. She didn't think he'd believe that she was in the habit of reading all those titles every month, and she wasn't quite ready to confess just how far out to sea she was. She'd wait to get a look at the house first, at least.

Cole was leaning on the railing of the open stairway with his back to the door of her apartment, his forearms braced on the banister, looking at something in the hall below. He was wearing a windbreaker, and running shoes, and jeans—not the designer-aged variety, but genuinely old ones that had been bleached out with repeated launderings until they were the palest of blues. It surprised her, though she didn't know quite why it should; even tycoons liked to be comfortable, surely, and there was nothing more comfortable than an old pair of blue jeans that had shrunk here and stretched there and softened and eased all over through hundreds of wearings until they fit the body....

And those jeans certainly fit that body! she found herself thinking. She had known from the beginning that he had a nice physique, of course, but then she'd never seen it before from quite this angle.

*Cut it out, DeMarco,* she told herself. *And stop drooling! The last thing you need to do is start psyching yourself into more trouble. He's quite capable of providing enough of it to keep you busy. Just keep things on a light note. The worst thing you could do would be to let him know that what happened last night kept you from sleeping properly.*

He turned his head and smiled at her. "Doesn't this bother you?" he asked. "The open stairway, I mean."

"Not if I don't drape myself over the edge as you're doing." She could see now what he had been watching; it was the starburst patterns of light that cascaded through the semicircular stained-glass panel above the front door. "Beautiful, isn't it? It's unusual to find such an elaborate piece of glass in a brownstone."

"Really? Of course, you'd be the one to know."

The expert, she reminded herself. Well, at least here she did know what she was talking about, and if there was a chance of pounding a little good taste into his head, she'd give it a try. "It's the best one I've ever seen. There's a guy from a salvage company in the city who would love to get his hands on that window."

"They do stuff like that?"

"You mean like taking windows out of perfectly sound buildings? Of course. And they don't stop with windows, either. Mantels, doors, copper plumbing, sinks—you name it. But fortunately Mr. Maxner owns this building, and he isn't interested in selling it piece by piece."

"Wise man."

There was a note in his voice that made Heather suspicious. "Which of them?" she asked flatly.

"Both." She made a face at him, and he grinned. "I've made up my mind not to argue with you today, Heather, so don't provoke me. Are you ready?"

"That's low. It's not my fault we're always arguing."

He tipped his head to one side and looked at her expectantly.

"It's certainly not *always* my fault," she amended.

"Whatever you say, darling." It was cheerfully agreeable. "No notebook or anything?"

"I'd prefer to get just a general impression the first time through." She hoped it sounded reasonable; she hadn't even thought of taking notes.

She eyed the sleek little fire-engine-red sports car at the curb. "No limousine today?" she asked. "I'm so disappointed." She folded herself up and crawled into the sports car, grumbling. "Don't hit any potholes. I'd hate to have this twist in my spine become permanent."

"You don't like getting into kinky positions, then?"

Trust him, she thought, to get a double meaning out of the simplest remark.

"By the way," he said, "are you certain that we weren't lovers in a previous life?"

*"What?"*

"You mentioned the possibility the other day. You see, I dreamed about you last night. It's the strangest thing, but I seem to know just what you'd like, as if I've learned it all a long time ago, and only need a little practice to get up to date."

She sputtered, until she saw the grin lurking in his eyes. So she turned her back on him and studied the landscape.

She had underestimated the car; it was like riding a cloud—or a rocket. Cole took the ring road around the metropolitan area, and before she had a chance to wonder just which section of the city his house was in, they were pulling off the freeway and onto a winding road that seemed to lead nowhere.

The car flashed past an intersection where a wide aisle of huge old trees led back from the main street toward a sprawling Southern-plantation-style mansion, and then Heather knew where she was. "That's the Century Club, isn't it?"

Cole nodded.

She thought he looked a little surprised that she had recognized it. "I might not move in the most exalted circles every day," she said acidly, "but I do read the newspapers. And I was there once for a wedding."

He frowned. "And I never heard about you being there? I must have been out of the country to have missed that story—"

"And you were accusing *me* of picking fights," she accused.

He took his hand off the gearshift, captured hers and raised it to his lips. It was a courtly gesture of apology, and she knew quite well it was rehearsed. She pulled her hand away with a little growl.

"Is it true that it's so exclusive that there are only a hundred members?" she asked, trying to take her mind off the spot on the back of her hand where his lips had rested. It was almost an itchy sensation—she wanted to rub it.

"It's true. Not that there isn't pressure for change, because the waiting list runs into the thousands. The Century Club is more exclusive than the Mayflower Society and the Daughters of the American Revolution put together."

"Do you belong?" Her question was casual.

"Sorry. I'm one of thc mere thousands who wait, humbly, to be summoned into the presence." He glanced at her. "You seem surprised."

"Amazed is more like it," she said frankly. "I thought with your money they'd be eager to have you."

"Did you?" He didn't sound interested.

The repressive note in his voice perversely urged her on. "Or does the Century Club feel that some kinds of money are better than others? You made yours all by yourself, didn't you?"

"Every penny of it. What are you up to now, DeMarco? Getting ready to write an unauthorized biography?"

"Yes, in my spare time."

"I shall duly guard my tongue," Cole said.

Heather wasn't listening. She had her nose almost pressed against the window. They had left the manicured golf course behind and turned down a broad avenue lined at intervals with huge elegant old houses. With every block that went by, she knew she was getting further out of her depth.

"This isn't exactly the sort of neighborhood where the kids have lemonade stands in the summer and the neighbors get together to drink beer and grill hot dogs on Saturday nights, is it?" she muttered. "And I'll bet there isn't a single potted geranium hanging from a porch for miles."

He smiled a little. "This whole area is called The Hundreds," he said, "because of the proximity to the Century Club."

"And the fact that most of the residents have vain hopes of someday belonging, I suppose." She looked up, feigning embarrassment. "Oh, I don't mean *your* hopes are vain, Cole. I'm sure when your newly acquired wealth gets just a little older—"

"I appreciate the reassurance, Heather," he said dryly. "You quite give me hope."

Heather settled back in her seat with a little smile.

A few blocks farther on, Cole turned down a well-disguised, twisting little lane past some obviously newer houses. They were of more varied styles than the older homes up on the avenue; there was still plenty of English Tudor and upright Georgian brick here, but there were also a couple of contemporary glass-and-steel cubes. All the houses had certain things in common, however; each was huge, each stood on a large and irregularly shaped lot, and each was obviously a mansion—or was going to be; nearly all of them were still unfinished.

One was only a framework of timbers stretching skyward, and even on this chilly Sunday morning workers were scrambling over the skeleton. Heather looked at it doubtfully, but Cole drove on by.

The other houses were quiet on this day of rest, but they were just as obviously not yet homes; labels were still stuck to the window glass, builder's vans were still parked by the front doors, and driveways were still no more than ruts carved in the hard-packed dirt by the heavy trucks.

Only a couple of places were obviously lived in. One of them actually had trees on the front lawn—two spindly saplings and a couple of head-high evergreens. The saplings were staked and wrapped to protect them, babies that they were, from the nibbling of hungry creatures. Each had no more than half a dozen tiny, brave leaves.

A couple of houses even had what could be called lawns. But the blocks of sod had not yet melded together into a lush blanket, and for now, until springtime warmth brought the grass out of dormancy, the front yards looked more like dull brown quilts sewn together by a careless hand.

"Well?" Cole asked. "What do you think?" Heather warily followed his pointing finger.

The car had stopped at the very end of the cul-de-sac. Directly in front of them sat a French château, well back from the pavement. It was huge, by far the biggest house on the street, stretching perhaps two hundred feet in length. There were two full stories, and a row of small, arched windows along the roofline suggested a third, partial floor. There were half a dozen chimneys, poking up above gables so steep that Heather couldn't understand how any roofer could have kept his footing long enough to install the red slate. There were towers; she counted three at the front of the house, and she could see at least one peeking up from the rear. And there was a two-story-high greenhouse that seemed to form a hallway between two wings.

She darted a glance at Cole. His hands were folded together at the top of the steering wheel while he admired his treasure. She smothered a sigh, and thought that all those magazines had been a waste of time and money; nothing could have prepared her for this.

The white stone facade was fresh and new—and raw, Heather thought. Each angle was too precise, each delicately carved bit of tracery too sharp, each slab of slate too bright. There was not a bush or a tree to soften the impact, or help to disguise the building's massiveness. It sat alone in a sea of gray-brown clay.

*And you have to work with it, Heather,* she reminded herself. *That is not an option.* "It's—the most incredible house I've ever seen," she managed to say.

The corner of Cole's mouth twitched. "You sound as if you're strangling. Stop biting your tongue and tell me what you really think."

"Well—you're right. Your ideas of beauty and mine do not agree." The words almost burst out. "Fifteen years might improve it. When it's had a chance to weather a little, it might look a bit less like a movie set. And some trees would help. But unless you're going to import them fully grown, it's going to look like hell for years, Cole. I can't believe you perpetrated this."

"You sound disappointed. Would you rather I'd built a scaled-down Dennison Tower?" It was a casual question, as if he already knew the answer.

"Yes," she said firmly.

He looked absolutely astounded. "I thought you hated glass and steel."

"It's all right in its place. And then at least it would have been real, not this plastic fraud."

"Plastic?" He sounded hurt. "I beg your pardon, but that's marble—"

Heather wasn't listening. "And it would have been *you*—unconventional and straightforward and plain-speaking, not trying to hide behind something you aren't. That's not a fake Monet above the mantel in your office."

He blinked at that. "Of course not. But what has my taste in art to do with anything—"

"And if you couldn't afford the real one, you wouldn't put up a copy. Would you?"

"Of course not. In self-defense, Heather, perhaps I should point out that the Monet is only a minor one."

"I don't care if it's a rag he used to clean his brushes—the point is it's real. This house isn't. It's a charade, and it's beyond me why you seem to think it's—"

"It wasn't entirely my idea, of course," he reminded her mildly.

She had, for those few minutes, utterly and completely forgotten that this was not his house alone. "Oh! I'd forgotten Elizabetta's passion for Paris," she said weakly. "Of course she wouldn't want glass and steel. But I'm surprised she didn't want to renovate a Winchester house, instead of doing this."

"There are Winchesters still living in all of them." He urged her toward the front door. "And none of the houses are in The Hundreds."

She resisted. "Cole, I can't pull off French renaissance—"

"Of course you can. It's just a matter of adjusting your mind to it. It's like switching from standard to metric measurements. You have to think about it for a while, but then it all clicks into place."

"But I don't have any experience with the style!"

"So check out a book at the library."

She rolled her eyes heavenward, and saw the fleur-de-lis carved in the keystone above the arched doorway. That single little detail steadied her somewhat. If the plans were so specific, then what could be left to be done inside? She would just approve the plans—

That reassuring thought did not last long. The arched double doors swung wide, and she stepped into—not a mere foyer, surely, she thought in desperation. No, this was nothing less than a grand reception hall.

It was huge, with a ceiling that reached almost to the roof, at least sixty feet above the main floor. Dust particles—and there were plenty of them—danced in the streams of sunlight flowing in from windows on all three levels. A twelve-foot-wide white marble stairway began at the main level and split into two branches at a landing halfway to the second floor; the room was so enormous that the span did not look oversize or out of placc. She took two reluctant steps forward and looked up; above the foot of the stairway, where some grand crystal chandelier should hang as the focal point of the room, there was not even a chain—just a dull white electrical wire handing from the ceiling, with a bare light bulb dangling from it. She sighed. That would be a challenge.

The floor was only rough plywood, and not even a banister rail guarded the staircase—only two-by-fours roughly nailed together and anchored heaven-knew-how to the marble.

"I suppose that's going to be gilded wrought iron," she said grimly.

"See?" Cole applauded. "You do know what you're talking about."

Off to the right was a series of large rooms, at present unfinished and unidentifiable. Despite the museumlike precision of the exterior architecture, the inside had an indefinable contemporary feel to it, with entire walls of glass toward the back of the house. Had they really built châteaus like that? She doubted it, somehow; it seemed to her like an uneasy compromise between two very different architectural styles.

"Drawing room," Cole said helpfully, "then billiards, smoking room—"

"You don't smoke."

"Well, it sounds better than calling it a poker parlor, don't you think? There's an exercise room and sauna beyond that, and as soon as the weather permits they'll put in the pool behind that wing."

She turned her back on him. That gave her a view of the room to the other side of the reception hall, an enormous space, rounded at one end. Of course, she thought. It was one of the towers.

"Dining room," Cole said. "Beyond that is the greenhouse and the garage wing and the helicopter pad."

"How many square feet?"

"Twenty-three thousand, give or take."

She was astounded. "Cole, that's ten times the size of the average tract house! What on earth do you need all this space for?"

He frowned. "To impress people?" he said hopefully.

"That's honest, at least. But you don't have to try to impress them, you know."

"Is that a compliment?" His hand brushed her cheek softly. "Thank you, darling. It's very thoughtful of you."

She gave up and started walking from room to room.

She had been prepared for bare floors, bare walls and the smell of sawdust and drying plaster. But she had expected that basic construction would be finished—and it was not. There were no doors between the rooms. There were holes in the walls where she assumed sconces were supposed to fit. There were fireplaces roughed in, but they had no mantels or surrounds.

And that was only the beginning.

She lost count of the rooms long before they left the first floor. There was a loggia that Cole assured her would one day have a lovely view of the pool. There was something merely called a round room. There was a nook—for storing logs, Cole told her—that was bigger than her apartment's bathroom. And the reception rooms and sitting rooms and drawing rooms and libraries went on and on, replicating themselves wherever she turned, until she honestly thought she was seeing double.

She was certain of it when she cautiously climbed the marble stairs and was shown through the master suite, which had a huge bedroom, dressing room and bath off each side of a big sitting room overlooking the as-yet-imaginary pool. Taken as a whole, the suite consumed half of the entire second floor and two of the towers, and included a walk-in closet with its own balcony opening off a set of French doors.

"This is the nursery, right?" Heather asked, standing in the slightly smaller bedroom. "Handy for three o'clock feedings and nightmare-soothing—"

"No, Heather," Cole said gently. "The house honestly has two master bedrooms. And it's a little early to be designing a nursery, don't you think?"

Well, there was plenty of room if he changed his mind, she thought. She wondered whose idea the two-bedroom suite was, originally. Elizabetta's, because everyone in her new level of society did the same? Or Cole's—simply because he always planned ahead? In any case, it confirmed her suspicion that Mrs. Cole Dennison wasn't likely to be the only woman in his life. "Aren't you even going to sleep together?"

"I don't like to shock you, but if you're talking about making love, Heather, sleeping doesn't have a whole lot to do with it."

"Don't be an idiot," she said crossly, without thinking. "Of course it does." She thought Cole's eyebrows were going to collide with his hairline, and felt herself turning wildly pink. But it was too late to back out now without making clear what she had meant. "Sex can be an isolated physical act," she said crisply, "but making love can't. Half of loving is simply cuddling up together. Reaching out to touch each other in the night. Going to sleep in each other's arms—"

"And waking up an hour later to snores?"

She said with dignity, "My mother told me once that's the worst thing about being a widow—waking alone. No sound. Not even a chain saw of a snore." She bit her lip and went on stiffly. "But then I suppose it's only my middle class upbringing that tells me that married people sleep together—the same life-style that gave me a taste for lemonade stands and potted geraniums and hot dogs on the grill. I certainly don't care what you do."

"Of course you don't," he murmured.

She retraced her steps across the sitting room into the larger bedroom. The sooner the subject was changed, the better, she thought. "This is Elizabetta's, right, with the cedar closets?" She didn't wait for an answer before poking her head into the adjoining bath, housed in one of the towers. It was the size of the average efficiency apartment; it even had a fireplace. But she'd been—unfortunately—right the first time she looked at it; the plumbing had been roughed in and capped, but there was not even a vanity sink to be seen. "This is a massive undertaking," she muttered. "It can't possibly all be done by the beginning of summer, Cole. That's only a couple of months."

He sounded just a little cynical. "You'd be surprised what can be done when you're willing to pay the price."

She turned her back on him and tiptoed down the stairs, her heart in her throat at the way the makeshift railing felt under her hand.

"Aren't you going to look at the third floor?" Cole called from the landing.

"As soon as there's a real banister in place, thanks. Before then, it would be too much of a temptation to push you off."

There was a smile in his voice. "I'm not worried. You couldn't get close enough to the edge to do it."

"Besides, I thought we were touring a mere house this morning, not the palace at Versailles. I barely have time to get to work."

She was dead silent on the way back around the city, chewing her lip and trying to decide if she was an idiot even to consider taking on such a massive job, one for which she was so clearly unqualified.

There seemed to be no question in Cole's mind, however, that she would do it. "I'll have the architect there at ten o'clock tomorrow morning to meet you," he began.

"I'm a working woman, Cole. Where do you think I'm going to make time between now and ten o'clock tomorrow morning to find out what sort of thing fits in a neo-European monstrosity like that one?"

"Oh, I'm sure Audrey will have some suggestions for you to consider. Places you should look, at least. She knows them all."

"Why don't you let Audrey take care of it, then?" Heather said sourly.

"She's a busy woman, too. And I'd end up with a winning entry in the architects' contest, but not a home."

"Nothing can make that place a home, Cole! It's ghastly. You said you wanted a back door—all right. But that house has nineteen of them."

"You're kidding."

"No, I'm not, dammit. I *counted*—"

"Just talk to Audrey, all right? It's only a preliminary conference, not some sort of a test you have to study for."

That was exactly what terrified her—that this was only the beginning. The sensible thing to do, Heather instructed herself, would be to tell him right now that she wasn't what he thought. He'd probably be glad she had confided the truth and saved him from putting his precious house into such precarious hands.

She was just drawing a breath to confess when the sports car made a neat U-turn into the parking spot in front of the brownstone, and she saw the crane in the school yard across the street. From this angle, it looked like a vulture, sitting there patiently. The wrecking ball was safely stowed, but it would take only a word from Cole, tomorrow morning, to unleash it.

*I hope Elizabetta decides to forgive him,* she thought resignedly. *Because once they make up their quarrel, she'll have me off the job in a minute. But I'll have fulfilled my part of the bargain, and so Cole will still have to keep his promise to renovate the school.*

*And I hope she makes it soon,* she told herself. *Before I have to go looking for a damned chandelier that will make the most of that ridiculous front hall....*

## CHAPTER SEVEN

TO HEATHER'S utter surprise, Cole didn't disappear back into the city, but walked down the hill with her to Cookys. "You said this is a wonderful place to shop," he said airily when she asked what he had in mind. "So I'm going to shop."

"For what?"

"Wrought-iron spiral staircases. I'm sure you'll insist that they be authentic, so I expect it will take me all afternoon to find thirty of them. Unless you would like each one of them to be unique. Then it might take a little longer."

"The rest of the week at least," Heather said dryly.

"If it takes too long, that would be another strike against your plan, I'm afraid. Perhaps you'd like to consider the concept of a minimum-security prison, after all?"

He didn't wait for an answer, of course, just strolled off jauntily down the street, apparently paying no attention to the sign on the wrought-iron shop across the street. Heather just shook her head and went to turn the ovens on.

There was no predicting Cole Dennison, that was sure. He might just disappear altogether, having accomplished some shady private purpose by making her expect that he'd be turning up at unexpected intervals all afternoon. On the other hand, he was capable of strolling into Cookys with a couple of hefty moving men and a complete staircase as a gift for her, and asking blandly where she'd like him to store it—just to keep her off guard.

She dumped the stale leftover bits of cookie out of the plastic fire hat, washed it and put it back on top of the display case as a reminder of what this acquaintance with Cole Dennison had already cost her. She probably would never have been more than friends with the young fire captain, but now she would have no chance to find out; any interest he might have felt had been blasted away. Meanwhile, Cole obviously was interested in her—but in all the wrong ways.

*You'd better remember that, Heather,* she instructed herself. *It will be a lot easier all the way around if you do.*

As it happened, Cole didn't turn up again till late afternoon. His hair was ruffled by the wind, and he looked extremely pleased with himself. Under his arm was a box, the size and shape that florists used to hold a dozen roses. But this box was corrugated cardboard, with ragged edges and bent corners and stained sides. It looked as if it had been stored for a long time in someone's attic.

Heather eyed it warily. From the look of him, she'd bet it was some sort of gag gift, but it wasn't big enough to be a spiral staircase.

But he made no move to offer the box to her. He merely set it down carefully on the nearest glass-topped table and came over to inspect the contents of the display case.

"I've been thinking," he announced. "Is your mother Cooky, or did she name the place for you?"

Heather considered the implications of the question for a moment and decided to play it straight. "Neither," she said. "Didn't you notice? There's no apostrophe. It's purely descriptive of the product."

He frowned. "Then it's spelled wrong."

"No. It's spelled *creatively.*" *And don't get upset about it,* she warned herself, *or he's apt to ask why you should be taking it personally.*

"Well, that's good. That it's not a nickname, I mean. I never understood why some women like to be called Cooky, or Muffy, or Pebbles, or—"

"That makes two of us. Do you want something?"

"Yes," he murmured. "But I'll settle for a sugar cookie. That one—it's the biggest."

The cookie he pointed out had a clown face painted on it with icing. Heather tried to always have a few of them on hand, because they were a favorite with very small children. "You are a surprise," she muttered. "Most people over the age of four don't eat those."

He bit deeply into the cookie. "Not bad," he said through a mouthful of crumbs. "Not quite as good as my grandmother used to make. But don't tell your mother. I wouldn't want to hurt her feelings."

She had to bite her tongue to keep from telling him that it wasn't Katherine who had put together those ingredients—or even dreamed up the recipe. "Cole, everybody's grandmother made the world's best cookies. It's a law of nature, just like gravity."

He shook his head. "No, my granny really did. Of course, she had a magic whachamacallit—a rolling pin."

"Magic? Oh, come on."

"I'd forgotten all about it till I found one just like it in a shop up the street." He opened the top of the box. "Want to see?"

"You bought a— You are joking, aren't you?"

But the object he took out of the box was indisputably a hand-carved wooden rolling pin. It was very old, very scarred and very dirty.

"Would you like to borrow it?" he said generously.

"Get it back in the box!"

Cole looked hurt.

"If a health inspector saw that thing and thought I was using it, he'd close me down in a minute." Heather eyed it warily. "Scrub it with bleach, and maybe it will be salvageable. What on earth is supposed to make it magic?"

"This one might not be. But my grandmother's worked in a flash, and nothing ever stuck to it. I used to watch her roll out cookies—"

"I hate to tell you, Cole, but that wasn't magic. It was years of practice. My grandmother was just like her."

"Oh?" He looked at the rolling pin with a disappointed air. "Well, it was still worth buying."

"I'll bet you paid a price that would have made your grandmother screech in pain, too."

He told her, and she winced. Then she reminded herself that the price certainly had not disturbed the state of his wallet much, and told herself briskly to stop feeling sorry for him just because one of her fellow merchants had taken advantage of his inexperience.

Now that was a rare thought, she mused. The picture of Cole Dennison as an innocent lamb, ripe for a fleecing!

It was a disturbing image, for reasons she couldn't quite understand. "So what are you going to do with it?" She couldn't exactly see it as the centerpiece of any of the elegant, upscale kitchens she had found pictured in those magazines last night. And a mere humble country kitchen would certainly not fit in that château of his.

*Thank heaven it's not going to be my problem,* she thought. *I'll be happy to let Elizabetta be the one who consigns Grandma's magic rolling pin to the attic!*

The woman who owned the wrought-iron shop came in for her afternoon snack. She nodded politely at Cole, but there was no friendly banter, not the kind that would have been likely if he had been in her shop. In fact, it was a suspicious look that she gave him, as if she still half believed that story about the baby.

Heather reached automatically for a seven-layer fudge bar and said mischievously, "I forgot to ask about the spiral staircases for the school. Did you two manage to locate a few this afternoon?"

The wrought-iron lady blinked. "Spiral stairs?" she repeated uncertainly. "That's the first I've heard about it."

Heather shook her head sadly. "And you were going to tell me you just couldn't find them, weren't you, Cole? Shame on you."

He had the grace to look slightly embarrassed. "I got sidetracked," he muttered.

"Stairs?" The wrought-iron lady was turning it over in her mind. "You're looking for spiral staircases? I don't have any on hand just now, but I can get some. How tall? And do you want to use them for real stairs, or just decorations—like to hold plants and figurines?" She pulled up a chair beside Cole's and sat down, ready to discuss the matter.

The look Cole sent at Heather promised reprisals later. She only smiled. He deserved the discomfort, and she could handle anything he tried.

So she was a bit surprised, at closing time, when he carefully packed up his rolling pin and walked her up the hill to the brownstone, and then didn't even ask if he could come upstairs, but only said goodbye.

And she was absolutely furious the next minute, when he leaned out of the little red car and added, "It's business tonight, and I can't escape it. I assure you nothing else could tear me away, Heather, because I hate it so when you look at me that way."

"What way?" she asked, and immediately wished she hadn't.

"Disappointed that I'm going," he said contentedly. "And obviously missing me already."

COLE DENNISON'S CHÂTEAU didn't look any smaller—or any better, in Heather's opinion—in the hazy gray of Monday morning than it had in Sunday's brilliant sunshine. Heather parked her car in front and wondered idly if she should leave a note under the wiper blade explaining that she was on business, just in case the neighborhood security people came by and towed the car away. It certainly wasn't the kind of vehicle that would ordinarily be parked in this block; the only other car in sight was a white Jaguar.

"Maybe they'll just assume I'm the cleaning help," she muttered. She'd have been far more comfortable in that role, that was certain.

She dug the key Cole had given her out of her handbag. Like most of the other things about the house, the key was big—nearly twice the average size—and heavy. But it turned easily and silently in the lock, and the perfectly balanced front door opened without a hint of sound.

The reception hall was no less overwhelming than she remembered it; in fact, without yesterday's friendly sunshine, it seemed even more forbidding. She sighed and wished she had waited in her car instead. The whole house was spooky; she hated to think what it would be like to be here alone at night.

She was in the billiard room, wondering if that was yet another euphemistic name or if Cole actually played billiards, when she heard footsteps by the front door. The sound echoed in the huge, unfinished hall, and she started down the long row of rooms to meet the architect who had created this impossible house.

A woman, slim and elegant in a black suit, was standing in the reception hall. "Miss DeMarco? I'm Audrey Hobart."

"I'm happy to meet you."

The woman had a firm handshake and a pleasant smile. "Cole said he'd already shown you through the house. What do you think of it, Miss DeMarco?"

*She believes it's a throwaway question,* Heather thought. *An easy icebreaker. She's expecting me to fall all over myself with praise, and I'm sure the sort of people she usually deals with—especially if she designs many houses in this neighborhood—do just that. But she's put me squarely on the spot, before I've even had a chance to judge her attitude. I can't lie to her. But I can't exactly tell the truth, either. For all I know, she's Elizabetta's best friend....*

And maybe, Heather reminded herself, that was why she was here today—so the word would promptly get back to Elizabetta that Heather was ruining her house....

She took a deep breath. "I'm sorry," she said. "But I may as well be honest. You'll know how I feel soon enough anyway, even if I try to hide it, and that would only make things uncomfortable in the long run. Very frankly, Ms. Hobart, I think this house is the most appallingly ridiculous thing I've ever seen."

Audrey Hobart's smile did not fade. "Cole said that you always spoke your mind. Well, let's get to work, shall we?" She led the way to the round room, which was tucked into one of the front towers. "This is my favorite corner of the whole house," she said cheerfully, and gestured toward the bench that had been roughed in under the windows. "Plus it's just about the only place to lay things out and look at them."

The civil answer made Heather feel even more like a worm. "I don't mean that I don't appreciate the quality of your work, Ms. Hobart," she began. "I think you've done a marvelous job of putting all this together so it flows well from room to room." She looked around, and added dryly, "And wing to wing, and acre to acre. . . ."

The corner of Audrey Hobart's mouth twitched. "Let me guess. You think it's a bit large for two people?"

Heather sighed. "I think it's a bit large for most political conventions, to say nothing of the average honeymooning couple!"

Audrey started to laugh.

Heather wasn't quite sure how to take that. Was this obviously honest amusement an insult in itself, the reaction of a supremely confident woman to one whose uninformed criticism meant less than nothing?

"I don't pretend to be anything but an ordinary sort of person," Heather said a bit stiffly, "so when I look at this kind of display—well, there's no sense in pretending. I've got no business here, and I'm sorry you're going to have to put up with me."

Ms. Hobart took the end off a long cardboard tube and shook out a sheaf of drawings. She dropped gracefully to the floor beside the window seat, and began to riffle through the sheets. "It's obscene, isn't it? The entire thing—all thirty-three rooms of it."

Heather's jaw dropped. "But I thought—you drew the plans, didn't you?"

"Yes, I did. That doesn't mean I agree with them. I tried to tell Elizabetta she was making a fool of herself, but she wouldn't listen, and so we're all stuck with the result. Now, I took the liberty last night after Cole called me of sketching a few things for you to look at."

Heather was hardly listening. "Thirty-three rooms?" she said faintly. *You shouldn't be surprised,* she told herself. *You're the one who was counting outside doors.*

"That doesn't include the baths, of course," Audrey said matter-of-factly. "There are seventeen of them. Let's start with the foyer, shall we?"

Heather seized the drawing. It was neither floor plan nor sketch; it was a finished perspective rendering of the reception hall from the drawing room doorway. The gilded wrought-iron banister had appeared, and the walls were brought down to scale with intricate moldings and chair rails. Blocks of pink and white marble covered the floor in an elaborate pattern, and above the foot of the staircase was a chandelier. It almost shimmered, even in the pale watercolors of the drawing.

Heather studied it. This didn't look anything like a quick sketch to her, but she wasn't going to argue. It was all right with her if Audrey Hobart wanted to do the actual work. She started to hand the drawing back with her approval, and then paused. There was something about it....

And another thing was bothering her, too; a rhythmic noise like the beat of a jazz drum was nagging at the corner of her mind. Heather would have sworn it hadn't been there a moment ago, and yet it sounded familiar.

A moment later, it grew in volume, and she gave a little groan as she recognized it as the distinctive sound of a helicopter.

This time she didn't feel that familiar little curl of anticipation at seeing him. Instead there was a kind of stew inside her, of annoyance and irritation and something else that she didn't quite recognize. Probably it was leftover frustration from yesterday, she thought.

*Did I really look disappointed when he left last night?* she wondered. *If I did, it must have been only because I didn't expect him to go away so easily....*

"Cole Dennison is the least-busy tycoon I've ever known," she fumed.

Audrey looked startled.

"Not that I know a lot of them, of course," Heather added hastily. "But if he wanted to do the damned thing himself, then why did he drag me into it?"

"Oh, he doesn't want to do it himself. He's very good at delegating responsibility," Audrey said dryly.

"Oh? Is that why this house looks so sickeningly much like a wedding cake iced in marble? And that must be how it escaped his notice that he owns a school, too."

Audrey Hobart's eyes brightened. "You know about the school? That's going to be an exciting project."

"I live in Archer's Junction." She leaned forward eagerly. "Are you working on the renovation?"

Audrey Hobart nodded. "I'm involved, of course. It's going to be quite a challenge to find the right use for it. Turning it into apartments or condos is impractical."

"That's what Cole said. But I think it's just because it was my idea."

The noise of the helicopter had died. Heather heard footsteps coming across the house, and Cole's voice. "Audrey? Heather? Where are you?"

*Good grief,* Heather thought, *the whole damned place is like an echo chamber!*

"In the round room," Audrey called back.

"Don't tell him which one," Heather muttered. "Make him look in all of them. That will take him half the day."

Audrey only smiled. "About the school—he's right, Heather. It can't be cut into enough units to support on-site management, for instance."

Heather shook her head in astonishment. "You mean the building isn't big enough? That's the first time I've heard anyone say that!"

"I'm afraid so. It would be prohibitively costly to provide special amenities like a pool and exercise room and racquetball courts for so few tenants. Yet the apartment conversions would be expensive, and people paying that kind of rent expect extra features."

"Audrey." Cole's voice was gentle. "Shall we not bother Heather with the details?"

"What if I want to be bothered with details?" Heather asked bluntly.

Cole smiled. "Then just look around, and you'll find plenty of them."

"Well, one thing you don't need is a security system," Heather muttered. "A burglar walking through this place would shake the chandeliers down— The chandelier! That's what was bothering me." She picked up the drawing of the reception hall and held it out at arm's length. "The chandelier you've drawn is too small. It's dwarfed by the room. We'll have to find a bigger one somewhere."

Audrey looked down at the drawing. Her jaw tightened, just a little.

Heather gulped. What had made her challenge Audrey, who so obviously knew her business? She couldn't decide if she was glad that Cole was there, or sorry that he, too, had heard that remark. It might turn out to be a classic blunder, the one that made it plain to everyone that she was an idiot where this sort of thing was concerned.

*And if I've messed up,* she told herself stoutly, *who cares?*

Cole reached for the drawing and studied it thoughtfully.

"It's Austrian crystal," Audrey said quietly. She was looking at Cole. "And it's the one Elizabetta sent home."

"You mean you've already got this thing?" Heather said. "It's not just an example?"

Audrey sighed. "I've been sending sketches and suggestions and pleas and threats to France for three months now, and the only things that have come back are the chandelier and a polite little note saying that Elizabetta preferred to wait till she could see samples instead of mere pictures. We've got the chandelier, yes."

*And you've got a big mouth, DeMarco,* Heather told herself and chewed her lower lip in consternation. Discarding a real—and obviously very expensive—chandelier was a whole lot different from erasing one and substituting another in a drawing. But it was a bit late to back down from her conviction; if the idea was a stinker, she'd just have to sink with it. "I still say it'll get lost in that big room."

"Oh, you're absolutely right," Audrey said. "I knew that as soon as I saw it. Still—"

*Elizabetta sent it.* The words practically quivered in the air, but no one said them. And Cole's expressionless face offered no hint of his feelings.

*It doesn't matter,* Heather told herself. *Hang the damned chandelier in the hall where Elizabetta wanted it. It will probably end up there anyway!*

But that wasn't honest, she thought. He hadn't asked her to try to read Elizabetta's mind; he'd said she should choose what she thought was best, and show it to him.

"Hang it in the dining room," she said finally. "It would be perfect there."

"You're right. We'll just have to find its big brother for the hallway. Somewhere." Audrey made a note to herself.

Cole did not comment, but Heather thought he looked rather pleased. She wanted to kick him. Was he approving the change? she wondered. Was he thinking that this sort of thing was precisely what would bring Elizabetta back to rescue her precious house? Or was he just delighted that he had succeeded in giving someone else the headache of making all these decisions?

In the next half hour, without moving from the tower room, Heather and Audrey managed to cover most of the main floor. They sketched out cove moldings and invented a new kind of door for the powder rooms. And by the time they had worked their way through the main rooms, Heather's head was spinning.

"Now about the built-in bookshelves in the library." Audrey was chewing her pencil.

"Shelves in a library," Heather mused. "What a novel idea that is."

"How far apart should they be?"

Heather ran her hands through her hair. She would have liked to tear out a few handfuls.

"Believe me, I know the feeling," Audrey told her. "It's overload. Take a deep breath and hang on. We're almost finished now."

"Make them adjustable. Or is that just too hopelessly middle class? Does he collect paperback westerns or coffee-table-size art books?"

"Neither," Cole said.

Heather jumped a foot. He'd been so quiet for the past half hour that she'd forgotten he was there.

"Adjustable will be fine. And I declare it time for lunch," Cole went on firmly. "You've got enough information to start, haven't you, Audrey?"

"Oh, yes. I can do the specs for the moldings this afternoon, and by Wednesday the carpenters can start installing them. I don't have time for lunch, though. I've got another meeting—the new state office building."

"I heard that you and John are doing that one, too."

Audrey nodded without looking up. She was still scribbling with her now-dull pencil. "A frustrating job, but it's good for the reputation."

*It certainly is,* Heather thought. *Even I've heard of that job, and the top-rated architectural team that's designing it. And I told her I hated her house!*

"What about the kitchen, Heather? Can we get together at the end of the week to look at cabinets and appliances?"

"That might be a problem. I do have to work."

"I'll call the showrooms," Audrey said. "They'll be delighted to let you look after hours."

So much for that attempt to dodge responsibility, Heather thought. "All right. Thursday."

"And you won't have to fight the crowds that way," Cole added. "You can concentrate on the choices." He looked amused, as if he'd read her mind.

Heather tipped back her head and looked up at him. It was a long way; she was still sitting on the floor, surrounded by a litter of drawings, plans and catalogs, and he looked incredibly tall and lean standing above her. "We'll be sure to mention your name," she said sweetly. "It might raise the price, of course, but I'm certain you won't mind that."

"It will move along quickly now, once we get going," Audrey said. She gathered up her drawings, handed Heather a stack of catalogs and said, with another flash of that beautiful smile, "It's nice to work with someone who can make up her mind!"

"You'd think she meant that I can't," Cole grumbled as Audrey vanished down the length of the house.

Heather tried to get up, but an hour of sitting on the bare, cold floor had left her stiff. She reached up for help, and Cole hauled her to her feet. His hands were warm and strong on her wrists.

"Maybe that's exactly what she meant," she said. "How could you sit here for so long and never even express an opinion?"

"Because you two were doing just fine."

"But doesn't it matter to you? I mean, surely you have preferences, Cole."

He shrugged. "I suppose I do, but I wouldn't know where to start. This is a whole lot more Elizabetta's house than it is mine."

A little stab of sympathy jolted through her. "And you can't see yourself living in it without her, can you?" she said gently. She had to clear her throat and try very hard in order to keep her voice casual. "I'll remember to put down thick carpets, by the way, so your kids won't have colds all the time— Oh, I forgot. No kids, right?"

"I didn't say I was never going to have children, just that it was too soon to start hanging pink and blue wallpaper."

"Well, two master bedrooms... I assumed..."

He began to smile, and raised both her hands to his lips. "Heather," he said. "Let me explain how these things work."

The soft warmth of his mouth against her fingers sent quivers along her muscles, such strong impulses that she hardly had enough control to pull away. "Oh, never mind," she said hastily. "I don't need another lecture on the birds and the bees."

"Whatever you say. Shall we go to lunch, then?"

A sensible woman would refuse, politely, Heather told herself. A sensible woman would go straight home and concentrate all her attention on the dirty laundry. A sensible woman would tell him to go jump out of a third-floor window....

"I should get home. I've a long list of things to do."

He raised his eyebrows slightly. "It's only lunch, Heather. Feeding you is the least I can do for all the work you've done this morning. And then you'll go home ready to plunge into your list."

It was matter-of-fact. Of course it was only lunch—a sort of thank-you. She was being silly. There was nothing wrong with going out to lunch with him.

"At Aphrodite's, perhaps?"

The newest, most upscale place in town, she thought. "I'm not dressed for that."

"Of course you are. We'll just dust you off a little."

A sensible woman would remember a couple of harsh facts, Heather thought. The first one was that there was a gulf between them. Cole was châteaus, and Heather was studio apartments. Cole thought in million-dollar multiples; Heather counted cookies. Cole was a three-course lunch at Aphrodite's, while Heather was a take-out sandwich from Ma's Deli.

And the second fact was that Cole Dennison's phenomenal charm could make any woman forget the first fact, if she didn't keep up her guard....

She tried to protest once more. "If you think I'm getting in that helicopter, Cole—"

"It's gone. Didn't you hear it go?" He tucked her hand into his elbow and chided, "And you were complaining about it being such a noisy house. Not very fair of you, I think. But I shouldn't complain when I'm hitching a ride, should I?"

He smiled at her, the smile that lit up not only his face but the entire surrounding area, and Heather's heart quivered just a little.

*You've got to be careful, DeMarco,* she warned herself. *You could so easily let this get out of hand.*

## CHAPTER EIGHT

HEATHER STILL DIDN'T particularly like Dennison Tower, but she no longer had to psych herself up in order to get into the elevator. Now it simply took a couple of deep breaths and the reassuring mental picture of the calm office suite waiting upstairs, and she was ready.

"Funny what ten days will do," she muttered to herself as she stepped out on the seventy-fourth floor and crossed the elevator lobby to the now-familiar executive suite. "Ten days, and a whole lot of trips up here."

The tote bag she carried was heavy today. It held samples of ceramic tiles for the master bathrooms and granite and marble for the kitchen counters, and her shoulder ached from the weight of them as she crossed to the secretary's desk. "Hello, Eileen. I believe Mr. Dennison is expecting me."

"He's down in the conference room, Miss DeMarco. But he said you may go on in and wait for him."

Cole's secretary seemed to be always the picture of cool efficiency, but every now and then Heather thought she caught a flicker in Eileen's eyes—of doubt, perhaps, or disbelief that the woman who had once broken into that office now had free run of the place. The first time Eileen had realized that Heather possessed the new combination to that door—and that Cole himself must have given it to her—she'd practically choked to death. Now it was obvious that she simply tried not to look whenever Heather punched in the code that let her into the inner office.

It was absolutely silent inside, isolated from the noise of the street and insulated from the clamor of the building. Above the mantel, the subdued blues and violets of the Monet water lilies seemed to shift and blur and call to Heather, and she took a moment just to stand there and look at the painting.

Only a minor Monet, Cole had called it. If that was so, then she wondered what standing in front of a major one—not in a museum under the eyes of a guard, but alone like this—would do to her.

She hummed as she arranged the tile samples on the coffee table and laid out the granite and marble on Cole's desk, and then she curled up on the little couch to wait for him.

It might be five minutes, or fifteen, before he returned, but she judged from the experience of the past ten days that it would not be longer. It had amazed her at first. Was this the man whose secretary had told her he didn't have a free moment for weeks? Then for a while she wondered if the opposite was true, if Cole was so easily accessible because time seemed to hang so heavily on his hands. Did the man have nothing better to do than sit in his office and wait for something to happen? But experience, and Audrey Hobart, had told her that neither was quite the case.

"It's not that he doesn't work hard," the architect had said just this morning. "The man holds the strings for an incredible number of enterprises. And it's not that he isn't willing to put his convictions on the line, either. But once Cole decides that something is important to him, he makes up his mind and puts the ruling into effect, so the problem doesn't have a chance to lie around his desk and nag at him. And then he goes on to something else."

Heather had nodded, remembering how promptly he had acted on the matter of the school—or at least, how promptly he would have acted had she not gotten in his way.

"But if he decides that it isn't all that important to him personally," Audrey went on, "he gives it to someone else to handle, and he doesn't concern himself with it anymore. That's why everyone I know likes working for him—there's real responsibility at Dennison Incorporated, and no boss breathing down one's neck waiting to pounce on a mistake."

Audrey had been looking around the château's still-bare master bathroom as she spoke, and she finished with a sigh, "Working *with* him—on something he cares about—is another matter entirely, I'm afraid. Do you think he'd like blue ceramic tile in here? There's a lovely sample in that batch you brought over yesterday."

Heather shook her head. "Green, I think. Dark green and cream."

"Though I will say he's been a lot easier to deal with since you've been on the job. You've been seeing a lot of him, haven't you?"

Heather was glad her face was practically buried in the tote bag, because she could feel a tiny tinge of pink creeping into her cheeks. "I suppose I have," she said, trying to sound careless. "There's an awful lot yet to do around here, you know." She pulled out a tile. "Here's the one I think we should use."

Audrey had taken it, and hadn't said anything more, but the look in her eyes had been skeptical.

That wordless expression of doubt had sent a little shiver up Heather's spine. *So it's not just my imagination,* she found herself thinking. If Audrey thought she saw it, too—perhaps it was really there. Perhaps it wasn't just the work on the house that made him drop in at Cookys to see Heather, or come by the château so often when she was there, or be so very accessible when she showed up at his office with a question.

*Perhaps it's that he really wants to see me, after all....*

It was not a new thought; the idea had been a delicious, tickling little notion curling around the edges of her mind for what seemed forever. But she had not let herself think of it long, or often. It had been too dangerous—too treacherous—even to contemplate. For the cost, if she was wrong, would be far too high. A sensible woman would not take the risk, and Heather was doing her best to be sensible.

And so, for the past ten days she had seen him almost daily, gone out to lunch with him, talked with him over drinks and told herself that it was no more than a business deal. She had let him kiss her now and then—mostly, it seemed, when he was feeling amused by something she'd said or done—and she had fended him off with humor whenever he had obliquely let her know that he really wouldn't mind at all if she didn't send him home at night to his lonely hotel suite....

"You should be sculpted, sitting just like that," he said.

She didn't even jump. He had come in silently, through the private corridor that he often used. But something in the most secret corner of her brain had known he was there, and so she turned her head slowly and smiled at him. "You're only saying that because you think if I was made of alabaster I couldn't do anything unexpected," she murmured.

"That would be a disadvantage. Come here." It was not a command, but a husky request.

She shook her head. "You're standing two feet from the window," she pointed out.

"That still bothers you?"

Heather shrugged. "Why risk it?"

Cole smiled slowly. "Because it might be fun to take your mind off the panic attack, now that I know what to do."

*This has gone quite far enough,* Heather thought. She bounded up from the couch. "I've got some things for you to look at," she said brightly. "And you'll be so pleased at the news. I just came from the house, and the moldings are all up, and the marble for the hall floor came—"

Cole had not moved. "You look pleased with it."

"I am. It's got a beautiful vein to it—"

"I mean the whole project."

"Because I'm not screaming about it anymore? Oh, there's a satisfaction in seeing the house take shape, I won't pretend there isn't. But I haven't changed my mind about it."

"I know. You keep telling me that house is a monstrous waste of good materials."

His air of long-suffering calm made Heather turn mischievous. "It wouldn't be quite so bad if it was devoted to a worthy purpose," she mused. "Perhaps you should turn it into a civic center. Or give it to the Century Club. Now there's an idea! With a clubhouse that size, they could take in the entire list that's waiting for membership—"

"How noble of you to take on that cause!"

She smothered a giggle. "Cole, dear, don't you know I'm doing it out of the goodness of my heart?"

He gave a little snort of disbelief.

"Sorry," Heather murmured. "I just get so overwhelmed I can't help myself sometimes. Actually, I expect that you'll give me something stunning as a token of your appreciation when I'm finished, and that's the only thing that keeps me going." She let her eyes drift wishfully toward the Monet, and then smiled sunnily at him and held out a plastic bag. "Try these. They might sweeten your disposition."

He seized it. "I can be bribed. Sugar cookies?"

"A new recipe. Or rather, a very old recipe. I found it in my grandmother's books." She watched, head tilted to one side, as he munched. "Is that what you remember?"

"Not quite. My grandmother's were a little tangier, somehow."

"That is an ingredient called Grandma's Love," Heather said good-naturedly. "It can't be duplicated."

He reached for another cookie. "How do you stay so tiny when you have all those cookies around?" he asked, munching contentedly.

"My mother was always handing out cookies to the whole neighborhood because I didn't eat them fast enough to suit her."

"Is that where she got the idea for her business?" The question was casual.

Heather bit her lower lip. *Tell him, Heather,* she ordered herself. *It's not fair to be still trying to hide behind that fake label of architectural historian—and not necessary, either. You've certainly proved yourself. He can't possibly object anymore to the fact that you're not an expert....*

He retrieved one more cookie from the bag and moved across to his desk. "What have we got today?" He reached for a piece of granite, hefted it experimentally and said, "Tell the truth, DeMarco. You're trying to put so much rock into this house that it will fall down of its own weight, right?"

She snapped her fingers. "What a wonderful idea!"

"Where does this go?"

"Kitchen counters," she said. "Granite doesn't chip or scratch or stain. And the marble is for the mixing center—it's great for rolling out pastry."

He grunted a little. "What's this going to cost me?"

"Plenty, I'm afraid. But it's worth it, Cole. You'll never have to replace those surfaces. And you don't even have to worry about a careless cook forgetting to use a cutting board."

"That is not one of my more vivid nightmares."

She smothered a smile. "I'm glad you approve. I'll order it this afternoon."

He had moved across to study the tile samples. "I'd have bet you already had."

"Oh, I wouldn't spend your money without your approval, Cole. At least, not in chunks that size."

He looked up with a challenging gleam in his eyes.

Heather decided a change of subject would be prudent. "Did you get my letter about the spring-cleanup weekend in Archer's Junction?"

"You know perfectly well I got it; you sent it to the hotel marked Personal, Confidential and Top Secret."

"Oh, yes," Heather murmured. "I'd forgotten."

"And half the staff was trying to read it through the envelope. They thought it was a love letter, the silly fools. I have referred it to the proper department, of course."

"That means Joe Hanford, I presume? Well, I suppose we can do without Dennison Incorporated this year, too." She reached for a block of tile. "I like this color best, myself. It's a bit more expensive, but—"

His eyebrows went up. "No wonder you like it so well!"

She took a deep breath. "Cole, I'm really not doing it on purpose, you know. Audrey is keeping running totals, but I'm not. I'd be terrified to know what this is costing."

"Then it's just as well you don't know, isn't it?" He kissed her cheek lightly. She held perfectly still until his lips, soft and mobile against the smooth skin, began to move toward the corner of her mouth, and then she turned her head away, a little too abruptly. "I really need to know what you'd like, Cole, so I can get the order in before this weekend."

"Oh? What's mysterious about the weekend?"

"Not mysterious—just busy. It's spring cleanup in Archer's Junction, and I'm in charge."

"I seem to remember hearing something about that," Cole said dryly.

"So I want to get ahead on your house, so I'm not keeping the contractor waiting."

"While you're raking trash. What fun!"

"As a matter of fact, trash or no trash, I'm looking forward to being outside all weekend. It's beautiful in the spring, Cole. The redbud trees are in full bloom, and the tulips are going to be early this year. Down in the ravines the jonquils are out and the bluebells are starting to flower..."

He looked perfectly sincere, but she could see a gleam in his eyes that spoke of unholy amusement. Well, he just didn't know what he was missing, she thought, up here in his climate-controlled aerie with his flowers made of paint and canvas!

"There's a whole row of flowering crabs beside the school, by the way," she finished. "They could use a little pruning, but otherwise they're perfectly healthy." She started to gather up tile samples. "How are the plans coming along, Cole? Or is it my imagination that there have been marketing people swarming all over Archer's Junction for the past few days?"

"How can you tell? They're supposed to be incognito."

"With those perfect haircuts and tailored suits? People like that stick out a mile in a district where everyone wears jeans so they can crawl around attics!"

He was frowning. "I'll remember that."

"So what are you looking for, Cole? Are you going to make it an antiques mall?"

He shook his head. "It would severely damage the existing retail blocks if I did. Another dozen storefronts could be absorbed easily, but thirty or more, all at one time..." He shook his head. "It's just too big, and the existing stores would be hurt by the sudden excess of space."

"The stores?" Heather asked. "Or the landlords? Do you mean the cost of rent might go down? I can't say I'd consider that a disadvantage!"

"The image of the community would change, I'm afraid. It would no longer be a crowded, successful, interesting little antiques district. It would look like a half-empty, desperate, on-the-edge-of-failure antiques district."

Heather frowned. "With the same number of stores."

"Absolutely. Public perception is an odd thing."

"Well, I can't say that I agree, but I see your point. What about a modern mall, then? Audrey mentioned the possibility. Is that the right way to put it? I mean adapting it for the sort of store that's in the suburban malls, instead of antiques. We don't even have a drugstore, as it is, or a shoe store, or a place to buy a greeting card."

"It's too small for that. And those businesses prefer new construction."

Heather wanted to scream. "Too big—too small—how can it be both? I know, Alice in Wonderland got in there somehow!"

Cole was grinning. "Sorry, Heather. I can't help it. Besides, I assumed you'd rather I kept the damned thing instead of selling it to a developer who might do anything at all with it."

"I'm not worried," she said stoutly. "You guaranteed me that it would be left there and made to serve a useful purpose."

"And you'd try to hold me to my word, no matter who owned it, I suppose."

The intercom on Cole's desk buzzed. Heather glanced at her wristwatch. Heavens, had she really tied him up for half an hour? She hadn't meant to, that was certain.

Eileen's voice was faint, but clear, through the speaker. "Mr. Dennison, Mrs. Winchester is returning your call. I knew you wouldn't want to risk missing her."

Mrs. Winchester? Elizabetta? *Returning* his call? *That,* Heather told herself faintly, *ought to be no surprise. But it is.*

"I'll be out of your way in just a minute," she said. "I didn't mean to keep you so long." She hastily picked up the last of the tiles.

Cole sat down on the corner of his desk, but he didn't pick up the telephone. "You do manage to keep my mind off my work," he agreed cheerfully. "If I ever find myself in need of an industrial saboteur, Heather, you'll be the first person I think of hiring."

The light comment gave her a queasy feeling in the pit of her stomach. She didn't answer, just caught up the bag and headed for the door. While she was still fumbling with the combination, she heard Cole say, "Hello, Elizabetta. I understand you'll be back in town Sunday." And then, a moment later, "I'd like to see you as soon as possible. I think we need to talk, now that you've had a couple of weeks to think things over."

Heather swallowed hard. The door opened with its customary soft swoosh, and she almost stumbled out into Eileen's territory and across the lobby to the elevator. For the first time in all her trips to his office, she felt no relief at leaving the seventy-fourth floor. She had a different sort of feeling altogether—a sense of desperation, of frustration, of anger at Cole . . . and at herself.

It was time for Cole and Elizabetta to have a talk, was it? *Now that you've had a couple of weeks to think things over....*

What had come after that? she wondered. Not that it mattered, really. It was plain enough.

The past two weeks had been only a holding pattern, Heather told herself. And she had been only a diversion, after all—something to occupy his time while he waited for Elizabetta to get over her snit and consider what she was throwing away, and calm down enough to listen. And now that he was back in touch with her, where did that leave Heather?

*Out of a job, for one thing,* she told herself. *It won't be my problem to see that ceramic tile installed, and I'm glad of it! So glad,* she thought ironically, *that I'm ready to burst into tears. And if I once start, I may never stop crying again.*

She could feel the sobs welling up inside her, painful and heart-wrenching. *You fool,* she told herself desperately. *You stupid fool, to let yourself forget all that!*

She had put Elizabetta and all she stood for entirely out of her mind, because she'd wanted to believe Elizabetta wasn't important to him anymore. And all the while Heather had been nothing more than entertainment—something to fill his time while he waited.

*He doesn't care about you, Heather—he didn't even care that you were there, and heard what he told her! You simply don't matter at all. He won't even remember you when this is over, unless, of course, someday he finds himself in need of an industrial saboteur!*

And what about Heather herself, and her feelings?

*I will never forget him,* she admitted painfully. *Because what I said about the house, in that joking tone, was true.*

She *was* doing all the work on his house out of the goodness of her heart. That was the problem, for she would be doing it, school or no school, simply because she wanted so much to please him. She would search the world for precisely the thing he wanted, just for the pure joy of seeing his pleasure in the final choice.

And the gift she would most like in return, as a show of his appreciation, was Cole himself. His humor, his joy, his concern—his love.

It was a kernel of truth that sprang up to haunt her despite all her efforts to bury it.

*There is nothing in the world you wouldn't do for him, Heather DeMarco,* she confessed. *Because you have fallen in love with him....*

When once she had begun to turn out the dusty secrets in the darkest corners of her heart, there was no stopping the cascade of unpleasant self-knowledge. She had been a fool—worse than a fool, because he had never attempted to conceal anything from her. She had walked into this with her eyes wide open, telling herself sanctimoniously that she was a sensible woman. And all the while she had been pretending that black was white, and that wishes were reality.

And now she would pay the price.

*Every good negotiation should end with a little pain on both sides,* Cole had said once. She didn't know if that was true, exactly, but it seemed unlikely that he would suffer much discomfort over this episode. While she...well, she wasn't coping with *a little pain,* either. This torment of the soul was pure and simple agony.

SHE DIDN'T KNOW if Joe Hanford had suffered a dramatic change of heart, or if Cole had issued orders, but there was a crew of men on the school grounds on Saturday even before the official starting time of the spring cleanup. Heather checked that job off her own list with a feeling of relief, and started to organize her crews to take care of the public areas.

"Rod and Brian, check all the parking areas for trash and soda cans." She balanced her clipboard on a post and started to apply sunscreen lotion to the back of her neck. "Jay—oh, dammit." The clipboard had slipped, and as she grabbed for it, lotion flew all over her.

A cool hand scooped up a blob from the sleeve of her flannel shirt and began smoothing it into her face. "Not a bad job, this cleanup stuff, after all," Cole murmured.

She had not sensed him there. *Even the chemistry between us has gone awry,* she thought almost sadly. She stood stock-still as his fingertips caressed her cheekbones, her forehead, her nose, until she could stand it no longer.

*Of course,* she thought. *Elizabetta won't be back until tomorrow—he said it himself.* And whatever they had worked out in that telephone conversation, it was obviously good news for Cole, for he was in the most buoyant mood she had ever seen him display.

*But in the meantime,* she thought, *he's got half the weekend to kill, and he's decided he might as well spend it with me. Well, I can't send him away. But I can put him to work, so he'll stay out of trouble.*

"Grab a rake, unless you brought your own," she ordered. "You can start in the little park around the corner."

"I only work under close supervision," he murmured. "So I'll wait right here till you can come and supervise."

"Cole, don't be ridiculous."

"I'm not," he said earnestly. "I haven't any idea what I'm doing. But as a responsible property owner I know it's my obligation to help."

She muttered something under her breath and set the rest of her crews to work. Then she took him around the corner to the little parklike area where they had sat and drunk their coffee and talked about the school....

*If only I had backed away that day,* she thought, *if I had given up my fight to save the building and simply gone back to work, none of this would have happened.*

No, she told herself. It had already started, and it had been too late to stop it. She had been as fascinated with him as it was possible to be, even then.

"Ah," he said contentedly. "Alone at last."

She moved to the other side of a bench. "That's not what you're here for, Cole. I'll be back to check on you later."

He leaned on his rake and watched her thoughtfully. "What's gotten into you today?"

He sounded surprised, she thought. Well, she had no reason to be annoyed by that, surely. It was sure confirmation that she held no real importance to him, for if he had thought of her with any personal interest at all, he would have been sensitive enough to understand. He'd probably forgotten that she was in his office yesterday, and had heard that conversation.

*And if he remembers,* she told herself, *he will realize just why you're in this blue mood—that you're grieving for him. You certainly don't want that to happen. It's bad enough to be in love with the man. It's sheer idiocy to go around with your heart on your sleeve. Just act normal, Heather. Act as if nothing happened yesterday.*

"Nothing's wrong with me," she said. "I'm just busy." And she went off to check, unnecessarily, on the progress being made in the parking lots.

She didn't see Cole for a couple of hours, and then her conscience drove her back to find out how he was doing.

That might only be a small park, but she should have sent a crew to help him.

There was a pile of trash by the bench in the center of the park, and in the far corner Cole stopped raking and looked up when she came into view. "I think I asked you once if every man who associates with you ends up doing crazy things. Now I know—yes, they do." He looked at his palms and winced.

"Blisters?"

"Not yet. But I think they'll be appearing any minute."

She didn't wonder. The little park looked as neat as if he had turned over every stone in the graveled paths. "Go and get something to eat. There's a sandwich buffet set up in Cookys. I'll send in a crew to finish this."

"And take away my pride of accomplishment?" But he put down his rake without hesitation and held out his hand to her.

*Act normal,* she reminded herself. *It certainly won't look normal if I refuse to sit with him at lunch.*

His palm was warmer than usual, and she could feel bumps at the base of his fingers. "You're right about the blisters," she said.

"Will you kiss them and make them feel better?" he asked mournfully.

Cookys was crowded with volunteers taking a break, and Heather and Cole ended up sitting on the window ledge, with paper plates balanced on their knees. After they finished, Cole took the plates over to the garbage can and came back with two cups of coffee and a handful of peanut crispies that he had charmed from Katherine. By then, the owner of the antique-lace store had taken his place on the ledge. "No room," Heather said with a shrug.

He stood there a moment and studied the problem, then handed Heather her coffee and nudged her to one side, sliding in between her and the edge of the window, with one arm around her for balance. Every time he nibbled at his cookies, his encircling arm pulled Heather more tightly against him.

*Behave normally,* she told herself. Making a fuss would only call attention to their closeness. It wasn't unusual, in these circumstances; there were people sharing chairs all over the room. So she bit her tongue and did not protest, though the entire right half of her body felt tingly from the contact.

He munched his last cookie. "Katherine," he called, "you ought to be a chain, you know. Have you ever thought about selling franchises? Think about it—a string of Cookys from here to the Golden Gate Bridge."

Katherine looked harried. "That would have to be a joint decision," she snapped. "Ask my partner what she thinks of it."

Heather suddenly became very interested in the dregs of her coffee.

"Partner?" Cole said gently. "You're a co-owner of this place, Heather?"

She nodded. "When my father died, you see, he left some insurance money, and Mother needed a job, and it looked like a good chance for me to work while I put myself through school, so we went into business together. And after I finished my degree, there weren't as many opportunities as I thought there would be, so—"

"There were no jobs for architectural historians?"

She shook her head. "For elementary school teachers."

Cole looked as if he were suffering sudden, excruciating pain. "I've turned my five-million-dollar house over to a full-time cookie baker?"

"I tried to change your mind. You insisted." Then it hit her. "You've got a five-million-dollar budget on that house? And I worried about those granite countertops? That means I can put gold faucets everywhere, and that chandelier Audrey found that I thought was just too much—and—"

"Dammit, DeMarco, it is not your house!" His words were little more than a hiss.

They felt like a whip laid across her face. "I am perfectly aware of that," she said hoarsely. "And I thank heaven for it every day. If you don't know by now how much I hate that horrible house—" Her voice gave out, and she pushed herself up from the window ledge, stalked across to throw her coffee cup in the garbage and said, "All right, guys, if you want to get done in time to celebrate tonight, don't sit all afternoon over your lunch. Who's going to walk the highway to pick up trash?"

But her mind wasn't on the highway, even as she acknowledged her volunteers. She was wishing that somewhere, someday, there could be a house—or an apartment—or a hotel suite—that she could share with Cole. She wouldn't even complain about a tent, for she could make that into a home, just as well as any other place. If Cole was there, she reminded herself. She swallowed hard, for that could never be.

She didn't see him again until the impromptu picnic that finished off the day. When he came up beside her, she was absentmindedly spooning potato salad onto her plate—potato salad that she didn't want and didn't plan to eat.

"I'm sorry," he said.

She bit her lip, hard. "Me, too."

"Can we be friends again?" It was scarcely more than a whisper.

The villain, she thought. For what could she say to that, except that of course they could be friends again? She gave a little nod.

His smile was like none she had ever seen before; it was like a quiet sunrise, warming and reassuring and peaceful, and more devastating than anything she had encountered in her whole life. *The man is dangerous,* she told herself. *I have never known anyone so egotistically sure of himself, so defiantly self-confident—or so utterly fascinating. So comfortably masculine. And so quietly hazardous to a woman's peace of mind. Even when I know that there's no future here, that I can only be hurt worse, I can't stop myself.*

So she sat with him as they ate. She was quieter than usual, listening as he chatted with the other half dozen people who shared the big old picnic table, wondering if he was bored by it all. He didn't sound it, but could he really be so engrossed in Mr. Maxner's memories of the street fairs Archer's Junction used to host fifty years ago?

"Not the sort of neighborhood I grew up in," Cole said, lavishly putting hot mustard on his third hot dog. "After my father died, and my mother went to work, we ended up in something that wasn't much more than a ghetto."

Perhaps that explained the château in The Hundreds, she thought. She didn't have to approve of it in order to understand.

And perhaps it explained Elizabetta, too. She, too, had made herself a name to be reckoned with in this city. They had that much in common, at least—

He was watching her with something in his eyes that was almost wonder. "Don't cry," he said softly. "It wasn't all that bad, you know—at least, I don't dwell on the bad."

He walked her home in the cool dusk, almost in silence, holding her hand. She savored the peacefulness of that stroll, knowing in her heart that though she would no doubt see him again, it would never again be like this. And when he turned on the steps of the brownstone and bent his head to kiss her, she did not protest.

*It is one last stolen moment,* she told herself, *because we can never truly be together. But for now—surely it is no sin to pretend.*

It was a long and tender kiss, as soft as a shadow, and yet it bruised her soul as no other touch ever had. He held her close and gently, and she shut her eyes and savored the solidness of him, and the scent, and that tiny electrical thrill that came with his touch.

There were a thousand things he could have said then, and she would have forced herself to laugh a little, and then she would have sent him away. If he had flattered her, or teased her, or played some fancy trick with double-meaning words—but he did not.

Instead, he looked down at her for one achingly long moment, and said, "I want so much to make love to you, Heather."

She nodded. It was not agreement, just acknowledgment of a fact.

"May I stay?" It was barely more than a whisper.

A sensible woman would not add to her pain, Heather told herself. *I know what I'm risking—my well-being, certainly, even, perhaps, my sanity. But those things are in danger already, because all I can think of is him. I've already hurt myself so badly that it can't possibly be worse.*

*At least I can have this one precious time. This scrap of loving. This memory, to hold forever dear...*

"Yes," she said calmly. "Yes, you may."

## CHAPTER NINE

THERE WAS A MOON that night, but it was just rising, and so the merest gleam of silvery glory trickled through the windows of Heather's living room, the oblique angle casting odd, unearthly shadows. She stumbled as the door closed quietly behind them, and Cole caught her wrist as she reached for the light switch. "No need," he said, and cupped her face between his hands.

His palms were rough against her soft skin. "You did get blisters," she whispered. "I should put an antiseptic on them—"

"Forget the blisters, Heather." His mouth came down on hers in a kiss that was full of knowledge, and certainty, and something that stopped just short of demand.

The dim light robbed her of the full use of her eyes, but Heather quickly found that there was no need for sight. There was instead a heightened, stunning awareness of his touch, of the sound of his harsh breathing, of the scent of soft outdoors that clung to his hair and his skin, of the taste of him as he invaded her mouth, hungrily caressing....

She gave a soft little sob of surrender, and he picked her up and carried her across the apartment and into her bedroom.

Here the moonlight was stronger. It cut his face into sharp silvery angles, and she could see the fierce gleam of desire in his eyes. But his touch was unfailingly gentle as he dealt with the buttons of her work shirt, and softer yet—if that was possible—as he kissed the tender skin at the edge of the wispy bra that had been concealed underneath. "Flannel and lace," he whispered against the soft hollow between her breasts. "You're a mass of contradictions—do you know that, Heather DeMarco?"

She shivered under that branding, possessive touch, and he maintained the contact while the tingling sensation grew.

She had thought once that it would be terrifying to make love with him, and she had been correct. It was almost as if he did know her already, every inch of her. He knew precisely how to caress her, how to stir her beyond all reason—just as, in some secret corner of her brain, she knew those same things about him. It was as if in truth they had learned it all long before, in some far distant time and place and life, and practiced it in their lonely separate dreams, until now, when they could once more create one perfect bit of heaven.

When she could finally bring herself to move again, Cole was watching her in the moonlight. He had propped himself up on one elbow, and his fingers were twisted in her hair, which spilled wildly across the pillows.

"I've wanted this," he said quietly, "since that day you broke into my office."

She nodded. She knew the feeling, and could recognize it now, for it had seized her that day as well, and it had been building ever since. She had wondered once, with half-horrified fascination, if he was going to propose that she have an affair with him, in trade for his saving the school; the idea would never have occurred to her, she admitted to herself now, if she had not already been half in love with him, and prepared to grab any excuse....

"I'm glad you didn't use it as a negotiating point," she said idly. "But...why didn't you, Cole? An affair to save the school."

He frowned. "Because things like this shouldn't have any strings attached," he whispered, and kissed her, long and hard.

It was a touching thought, and yet, when she turned it over in her mind it terrified her. For he was, above all things, a man who wanted no strings attached to anything he did. No promises. Even his wedding vows, she suspected, would not mean quite what other men meant when they spoke those words; she could not forget those two master bedrooms at the château, and her increasingly strong suspicion that it was Cole who had suggested them.

*Even his wife,* she thought, *will have no more of him than I do right now—for this moment. For tonight...*

And so she hugged him almost fiercely close, and hid her face against his chest, and savored the strong beat of his heart against her cheek. It formed a rhythm for her thoughts. Long after he had drifted off to sleep she lay there, pressed close against him, and yet a million miles away.

*Tonight,* she was thinking. *There is only tonight....*

She didn't know she was crying until his hand came to cup her cheek and smooth the tears away. "I was snoring, right?" he murmured. "And you can't stand the noise after all."

She shook her head vehemently and tried to smother her tears, but it didn't work; she had lost control now, and all she could do was sob.

Couldn't he ever take anything seriously? she wondered in exhausted irritation. Did he have to make everything into a joke? Did that, too, come from his childhood? He had said something last night about refusing to dwell on the unpleasant things. Was this the defense he had used against the bad memories?

Cole's mouth touched her temple gently. "Do you want me to go, Heather?"

She gulped back a sob. It hurt her throat. "No," she whispered. "Oh, no—"

His fingers stroked her hair. It was not meant as a passionate gesture, she thought, but to soothe, as one would try to comfort a child. But his merest touch set off a raging storm inside her—a cyclone of sensation that threatened to swamp her—and she arched against him and cried out, a begging, wordless little plea.

When at last the storm had receded and left them both spent and silent, she drifted off, cradled in his arms.

But she frowned a little even in the depths of her sleep as she tried to absorb all she could of closeness, to keep her company in all the tomorrows yet to come—days, and nights, when he would not be beside her.

IT WAS FULL LIGHT when she woke, and she lifted her head gingerly to check the time on the bedside clock. It was later than she had thought possible. The cleanup crews would be gathering again in an hour or so, and she needed to be down on High Street before that, she knew. But still she didn't slide out of bed immediately. She eased herself up on one elbow instead, and lay very quietly to watch him sleep.

*No one could begrudge me these few precious minutes,* she thought, *alone with the man I love.*

Cole was sprawled on his back, one arm bent above his head, his face turned away from her. *It looks as if he's trying to escape,* she thought, *or pretend I'm not here. And a moment ago when my head was on his shoulder and my arm was across his chest, it must have looked as if I was trying to hold him captive....*

It was like a dash of cold water in the face, and once that awkward view of things had intruded itself upon her, there was no tucking it neatly back into the closet. There was an unpleasant little fluttering in the pit of her stomach, matched only by the cartwheel in her brain.

*You're a fool,* those uneasy twin voices chorused. *You're a fool. Just what have you accomplished? You could have sent him home last night, and kept your dignity and your self-respect intact. Was it worth it—one short night with him in your bed? And what happens when he wakes up, Heather? Do you plan to hang around his neck and wait until he makes it clear what last night meant—or didn't mean—to him?*

And how could it be more apparent, anyway? He could not have said more plainly that he wanted no strings attached. *What are you waiting for?* she asked herself. *For him to be brutally cruel, instead of merely honest?*

She slipped away from him; he groaned a little and turned onto his side, and his hand reached out to stroke her pillow. Heather stood beside the bed for a moment and watched him, and told herself to remember this as if it were a photograph—the look of him, and also the fact that a bag of feathers seemed to keep him just as contented as her presence had. More so, perhaps, for bags of feathers didn't wake up in the night and cry....

She found her clothes and tiptoed to the bathroom to get dressed, and she was in the kitchen writing a note to leave next to the fresh pot of coffee when he spoke behind her. "I thought the cleanup was finished," he said. He was eyeing her well-worn plaid flannel shirt.

She jumped, and her pen spun out of her hand and made a dark streak across the pale blue of her jeans. She wiped at it, futilely, but without concern; if it had not been for the stain, she would have had to find some other excuse not to look at him. That first fleeting glance she'd gotten hadn't been reassuring. He looked a bit like a pirate this morning, with half a frown and a stubbly beard and yesterday's crumpled clothes.

*So obviously he wasn't expecting me to come back with coffee to drink in bed,* she thought, *or he'd have stayed there. Or perhaps it was that he didn't want me to come in, with all my expectations of what the morning after should hold, and so he hurried and got dressed before that could happen....*

She told herself briskly that there was no sense in being a masochist about it. There was going to be plenty of pain as it was; she certainly didn't have to go looking for new hurts, and then run them over and through and around her heart until it bled.

"The cleanup," Cole prompted.

"Oh, we'll find plenty of things to do. Pruning the trees along High Street. Painting the park benches. Planting spring flowers, now that the beds are all cleared out."

There was no reason on earth for that last innocuous statement to bring hot color to her cheeks, but it did. She waited uncertainly for his comment; she didn't know what it would be, but she knew from experience that it was likely to have a pointed double meaning to it.

"That sounds like the fun part," he said quietly. "Much better than yesterday."

A wave of misery washed over her. *Make up your mind, DeMarco,* she told herself angrily. *You wouldn't have liked it if he'd made a punch line of it—but you like it even less when he stops sharing those devilishly funny insights of his. It makes you feel smaller, somehow, and a whole lot less important.*

He reached over her shoulder for the note she'd been writing to him. She'd gotten only as far as "Coffee is ready, cups are in the—" when he came in. It was no literary masterpiece, that was sure.

He read it and glanced at the clock. "I need to get back to the hotel."

He sounded almost guilty, she thought, for not helping again today.

"I have a business appointment at noon." He ran the back of his hand across his jaw, and smiled wryly. "And it's going to take a little effort to look presentable."

Yes, it was guilt she had heard in his voice, she concluded. But it was not there because he was backing out of the work.

*Don't lie to me, Cole,* she wanted to say. *I know it isn't business—it's Elizabetta. Don't you even remember that I was right there while you talked to her?*

But she didn't. Instead, she said, "On Sunday? Nothing serious, I hope."

There must have been a sharp edge to her voice, for he looked at her a bit warily, as if afraid he'd been caught. "It might be. I'll call you later."

She turned her head, and his kiss brushed her cheek—a mere cool touch of the lips—and he was gone.

She stood in the center of her kitchen, gripping her pen until the barrel bent, her knuckles aching with the pressure. So that was all, then. A magical, passionate night had given way to an illusion-free morning—for both of them, obviously. And Cole hadn't been able to wait another minute to get away. It was over.

"Sorry, Cole," she said, through teeth clenched against the pain. "I'm afraid I'm going to have plans for later. Just in case you call—"

She doubted that he would.

IT WAS ALMOST MIDNIGHT when she got home. One thing had led to another, and half of the cleanup crew had ended up at a pizza parlor after the work was done. They drank beer, they put away pepperoni and cheese as if they were the original plague of locusts, and they argued about everything from politics to religion to whether Archer's Junction was ever going to join the modern world—and whether it should try. That led to the school and a discussion that nearly ended in a fistfight.

"You ought to have left well enough alone," one belligerent man told Heather. "We were going to get rid of that eyesore, but you had to step in, and now look what we've got! You save the school, all right. It's still sitting there all boarded up, and nothing's going to happen for the next hundred years, either. So much for your influence with Cole Dennison!"

There was a nasty twist to the words, and it brought back all the doubts she had ever had. It also reminded her that in the past few days even Audrey had been shaking her head whenever Heather brought up the subject of the school.

She smothered the suspicions as best she could. Cole had given his word, hadn't he?

But she had half-seriously asked for that promise in writing, and she had never gotten it. There was nothing that really committed him to doing anything at all—just her word against his. And who, after all, would take her word for something, against Cole Dennison's?

*They're working on the school,* she reassured herself. *There are always people up there.*

*But nothing seems to be getting done, really,* she reflected. They'd put a few patches on the roof, and they'd pulled some plywood panels off the windows, and they'd repaired a little glass. A thousand dollars' worth of materials, and a couple of workmen plodding along, and it kept people from wondering if Cole had serious intentions at all. It was a good return on a very small investment.

*It all takes time,* she argued. *It would be insane to start remodeling and renovating without a plan! He has to know what direction he's going first, before it makes sense to do anything at all.*

But what possibilities were left? All the plans seemed to be falling through. She didn't doubt that he had looked for options; there seemed to have been a good many experts up there looking the place over day after day. It was just that they all seemed to be shaking their heads in despair most of the time.

She stayed silent, in the end, and let the argument rage among the others present. Perhaps the belligerent man was right, she thought. Perhaps she should have stayed out of it all. It might have been better for Archer's Junction, in the end.

And there was no doubt it would have been easier on Heather herself.

Easier, perhaps, she told herself. But better? Would she rather have missed knowing him altogether, in order to avoid this pain?

At the moment, she didn't know.

The fire captain took her home. As he walked her upstairs he told her they'd caught the hoodlums who had set the school on fire, in the act of torching an abandoned building in the next suburb.

"That's good," she said. She could already hear the telephone ringing inside her apartment. It sounded angry, she thought, and then told herself not to be silly; telephone didn't have feelings.

"You'll tell Mr. Dennison, won't you?" he asked almost anxiously. "I'm sure he'll be relieved to know."

Heather nodded. If she hadn't been so weary, she might have tried to be flippant, for it was painfully obvious that he thought it must be Cole who was calling. He could scarcely wait to get away.

The telephone had stopped ringing by the time she got inside, and only silence echoed through the rooms. It did not ring again.

She soaked in the bathtub for a while, and then dropped wearily into bed, hoping for an oblivion that did not come.

HEATHER HAD an appointment to meet Audrey at the château on Monday morning, and she had made up her mind in the wee hours of the night not to keep it. There was no point in it, after all; it was obviously not going to be her job much longer. That might even have been why Cole had been trying to call her last night.

But at the last minute she grabbed her car keys and started out anyway. Until she was officially told that she was off the job, she was still responsible, she told herself. And this whole mess certainly wasn't Audrey's fault. It would be rude to stand her up without an excuse.

"I could have just called her, if Cole had used basic common sense," Heather muttered as she drove along the beltway, faster than usual. "Five million bucks for a house, and he hasn't bothered to install a telephone in it yet!"

Audrey's car was already parked in front, among a variety of workmen's vans. The plumbers were starting on the bathrooms, Heather saw. A delivery truck was unloading as well. The workmen slipped as they carried a box down the ramp, and almost dropped their cargo into the side of a black Porsche. They caught it in time, and one of them stopped to wipe his forehead in relief.

Heather chewed her bottom lip. She didn't know anyone who drove a black Porsche.

She held the front door for the workmen and watched them start carefully up the stairs with their precious cargo.

Voices pulled her reluctantly down the long run of rooms, through drawing room and billiard room—it reminded her that she had never found the opportunity to ask Cole if he really played—to the smoking room. There were two feminine voices, and one of them was certainly Audrey's soft contralto. But the other?

Audrey saw Heather first, and gave her a strained smile as she came in. Then the second woman turned around. She was taller than Audrey, and slimmer. She was wearing long, sleek, flowing dark jade trousers, a softly tailored short jacket in the same shade and a matching scarf wrapped about her head like a turban.

*I know what happened,* Heather thought. *She got drunk and shaved off all her hair while she was in France, and that's why she's always wearing the odd headgear!*

"Well, if it isn't the little mama," Elizabetta said gently.

Audrey's eyes widened, but she didn't comment.

"I assume you've come to return the rest of the samples, and to pick up anything you might have left lying around my house." Elizabetta's voice was quietly cultured and calm. "I believe you have a key, too. Please return it today."

It was no more—or less—than she'd expected, Heather told herself sternly. So there was absolutely no reason for the desire in her heart to do black murder. It certainly wasn't fair to blame Elizabetta for it. Heather had to respect her ability to stay calm in such a difficult situation; if the positions had been reversed, she would have been clawing Elizabetta's eyes out by now.

*No,* she reminded herself. *Elizabetta doesn't need to claw me. She won.*

She glanced at Audrey. There was dismay in the woman's eyes, but that was no relief for Heather. If Audrey had known it was not true that Elizabetta and Cole were now reconciled, she would have protested. If she hadn't been told about the reconciliation, she would have looked shocked, and would have started to ask questions. So it was true. They had reconciled, and everything was back to normal.

"You're quite right, Elizabetta," Heather said coolly, and pulled the oversize key from her pocket. She had hated that key, but still it was like giving up her right arm to hand it over. She had hated the house, and its pretentious splendor, but still there had been a challenge in taking on the problem, and a feeling of accomplishment in solving it. "I hope you'll enjoy the fruits of all my labors," she said sweetly.

Elizabetta's precisely arched brows went up. "Some of it isn't bad," she conceded handsomely. "I'll have to rip a great deal out, of course, but on the whole Audrey succeeded in keeping you restrained."

Heather considered dropping the tote bag of tile samples on the woman's toes in retaliation. Instead, she meekly set it down in the corner of the room. "You'll have to ask Cole for the samples for the kitchen counters," she said. "I'm afraid I left them in his office on Friday. I had other things on my mind at the time."

The instant the words were out, she regretted them. *If you can't do better than that feeble effort, DeMarco,* she scolded herself, *you ought to know enough to stay silent altogether. It would take a lot more than the thought of you to upset that cold-blooded female.*

She was right. Elizabetta only smiled and said gently, "I'll be certain to ask him about it tonight when he takes me to the Century Club's initiation meeting."

*So she's pulled the strings to get him into the Century Club,* Heather thought with reluctant admiration. Well, it figured. Jack Winchester must have belonged, and it would have been awfully untidy if Cole weren't welcome at all of Elizabetta's favorite haunts.

Heather retreated in disarray, her embarrassment soothed only by the knowledge that Elizabetta didn't notice. She was already giving Audrey instructions about the crystal chandelier.

So Cole had been right after all, Heather thought. He had Elizabetta's psychological profile figured out down to a gnat's hair, and his timing was right on the money, too. They'd patched it all up, and it had all worked out just fine.

She couldn't help but wonder, though, if Cole had found it necessary to beg and plead after all—or if it had been Elizabetta who had done the surrendering.

SHE HAD BARELY put her apron on, and Katherine was still taking hers off and tidying her hair for her lunch date, when the telephone rang. "Cookys," Heather answered it absently. "May I help you?"

"Heather." His voice was husky. "I tried to call you last night. You weren't home—"

"I thought I told you I had plans." She tried to keep her tone light, uninterested, as if it didn't matter enough for her to remember whether she had told him or not.

He said grimly, "I need to talk to you. Have lunch with me."

"I can't, I'm afraid. I've missed far too much time at work."

"This afternoon, then."

"That's no better. I can't leave, Cole. Mother isn't feeling well, and—"

Across the room, Katherine blinked in surprise. She not only looked the picture of health, but—at the moment—appeared offended at the slander. Heather turned away and took the offensive; there was no sense in letting this drag on. "If you want to tell me about Elizabetta and that I don't need to work on the house anymore, there's no need—I already know."

There was an achingly empty silence, with not even the sound of her heartbeat to interrupt.

"Well?" he prompted. "What do you think?"

It was like a knife in Heather's back. *How dare he ask for my opinion—my approval?* she asked herself wildly. "It was no more than I expected," she said. Her voice was level and cold. "But surely it doesn't matter what I think. I've got customers, Cole. Goodbye."

In less than ten minutes he called again. "Are the customers gone?"

"No. Why are you calling me at work, anyway?"

"Because at least when you're there you have to answer the damned telephone," he said grimly.

"I told you—I was out last night."

"You don't want to talk to me, do you? Why not, Heather? Wasn't I as good in the sack as you expected?"

That would be the first thing he'd think of, she told herself. "No," she said as lightly as she could manage. "You're far better."

"Then what's your problem?" he said impatiently. "You can't behave that way and then just walk away from it, Heather—"

The blood was drumming in her ears. Was he proposing that they keep this sizzling little affair going? she wondered. A stolen night here and there in her apartment—or did he intend to sneak her into the château? She knew that house well enough to get away with it, that was sure, and there were those nineteen doors, so no one could possibly keep track of who was coming and going.

This time she didn't even bother to say goodbye.

It was midafternoon on Tuesday, and it felt as if closing time would never come. Tuesdays were almost always slow in Archer's Junction; the weekend traffic had died off, and the day-trippers usually bunched into the end of the week. But this Tuesday had been especially quiet. Katherine had taken the afternoon off because of the slump in business, and Heather had had far too much time to think.

*That gets you into lots of trouble, my girl,* she told herself. It let crazy notions take root, like the idea she'd got into her head that no matter how insane his suggestions were yesterday, she shouldn't have hung up on him. She'd almost got herself convinced that she should have gone to lunch with him, and let him explain....

*You know why you're thinking that,* she lectured herself. *You just can't stand for it to be over, and you'd rather lie to yourself, and let him lie to you, than admit you're a fool. The truth is he could charm you back into his pocket in sixty seconds flat, Heather DeMarco.*

The school day ended, and precisely seventeen minutes later Rod and his gang of friends arrived and settled down with their afternoon snack to tease Heather. But a few minutes later Rod came over to the display case, looking concerned. "You're not looking so good, Heather."

"Thanks," she said dryly.

"I mean—you're not enjoying being teased like you usually do."

"I love it, Rod," she snapped. "It's certainly better than heavy-handed sympathy!"

Then she felt even worse, because of the hurt in his eyes. How many options did she have, after all? She could keep behaving like a wounded bear, driving away business and fueling suspicions that there had been something going on all along between her and Cole or she could pretend that things were normal, and exert an effort to be her normal self. With time, it might even come to be true.

So when the next batch of cookies came out of the oven, she took a plateful over to the table. "Here you are, guys. Enjoy."

*"Free?"* Rod said, and looked even more worried.

Heather punched him lightly in the shoulder. "That's to give you all enough energy to move. Don't you have anything better to do than hang around here?"

He grinned. "We're the best advertisement you could have. Look at us, the picture of strength and health, and it's all due to Cookys!"

The owner of the wrought-iron shop came in for her snack. Heather packaged it for take-out, and was making change when the woman said, "I guess your tycoon friend isn't going to need all those spiral staircases after all, is he?"

"How should I know?" The retort came out a bit crossly.

"Well, it's a good thing I didn't actually buy them. But I know where there are at least a dozen. It's a shame to lose that kind of a sale." She took her fudge bar out of the bag and bit into it.

Heather nodded absently. Then it hit her. "Why do you say that? Nobody knows quite what he's going to do with it yet, do they? I mean, I don't think he knows himself for certain."

The wrought-iron lady shrugged. "I can make a good guess. The guys from the salvage company stopped in my store a while ago. They were on their way up to the school."

"To see what's needed for the rehabilitation, I suppose?" Heather prompted.

The woman shook her head. "To start removing the roof. Those tiles are hard to come by these days, you know."

There was a dead silence in the shop, except for the wrought-iron lady smacking her lips over her fudge bar. Then Heather whispered, "He's going to tear it down, after all." She was white to the lips, and the blood pounding in her ears sounded like a hurricane.

*Damn him,* she thought. *I told him about that salvage company myself, and now he's used it against me.*

## CHAPTER TEN

*HE'S DOING IT on purpose,* she thought helplessly, *to get even with me for rejecting him.*

But if he had decided to tear it down just to put her in her place, she thought, then why hadn't he simply brought back the crane and the wrecking ball? It would certainly have been a more dramatic gesture, and a faster finish. And she could hardly have missed that message.

*And what difference does it make to him what you think about it, Heather?* she asked herself. *Don't get big-headed—you're simply not important enough to him that he even cares what you want. You never were.* He hadn't promised to save the school out of some wish that she'd like him better for it, but because the deal benefited him. And now that it no longer did...

*I should have expected this,* she told herself. *I certainly know how promptly Cole can act, once his decision is made, and I ought to have known that he was capable of doing this.*

But she hadn't seen it coming. Despite it all, she had trusted him to keep his word.

And why shouldn't she have trusted him? she asked herself bitterly. He hadn't broken any promises before! Of course, that was because he had never made any personal guarantees to her, so there'd been nothing to break. If there was one thing that had been implied from the beginning, it was that Elizabetta would be back in his life. And he'd certainly made good on that promise.

And as for his assurance that he would save the school, and make certain it served a useful purpose—well, promises easily given were easy to forget. Or was it possible that he didn't see this act as breaking his promise? Might he honestly think that salvaging the materials was a satisfactory way to handle the destruction of a landmark?

*As if it makes any difference to me whether he takes it down and sells it off piece by piece,* Heather thought bitterly, *or crumbles it with a wrecking ball and uses it to fill some hole in the ground! The real treasure—the building itself—will still be gone....*

"Are you sure they're taking down the whole building?" she asked urgently. "The roof leaks. Maybe they're just pulling up the tiles and salvaging them to be put back when the repairs are done."

The wrought-iron lady shrugged. "All I know is they were practically drooling over the oak beams in that place. Some of them are probably forty feet long. You can't get stuff like that now."

Heather's heart thudded to her toes. "Except at salvage yards," she agreed.

"And the bricks—do you know what used paving brick sells for these days? I'll take another of those bars, Heather. Chocolate always makes me feel a little better when a big sale like that one disappears out the door. Thirty spiral staircases...I wonder if he's going to build something new, or just level it."

Heather ignored her.

Rod was hanging over the display counter, looking just as green around the mouth as Heather felt. Half a cookie dangled in his hand, forgotten. "What are we going to do now, Heather?"

She shook her head helplessly. There was nothing left to do, she thought.

"You're not going to give up now, are you?"

The challenge braced her a little. "Well, I can at least find out what's going on," she said, and reached for the telephone.

Audrey Hobart was in her office, and her secretary put Heather's call straight through. *Audrey must have forgotten to tell her that I'm no longer an important client,* Heather thought. "Audrey—" she began.

"I'm so sorry about this morning, Heather! It was a shock to me, too, you know, when Cole told me. And I'm sorry Elizabetta had to be so catty about it. I'm not looking forward to dealing with her again, you know. I've been thoroughly spoiled by working with you—"

"Audrey—" Heather's voice was a mere thread, and she had to try again. "That's not what I'm calling about. It's the school. What in hell is he doing up there? They're starting to tear it down!"

There was silence on the other end of the line. Not shocked silence, Heather thought, but uncomfortable, uneasy, trying-to-think-of-how-to-explain-it silence.

"What is it, Audrey?"

There was a long sigh. "Heather, Cole has asked me not to talk to you about the school. If you want to know what his plans are—"

"Dammit, Audrey," she said flatly, "yes or no—is Cole planning new construction on the site of the old school?"

"Well... yes. But—"

Heather closed her eyes in pain.

"If you'd talk to him, Heather... It's all so very complicated...."

"Thank you, Audrey. Certainly I'll talk to him." Her tone was crisp, and she slammed the telephone down, hard.

*I've been conned,* she thought. *And I almost felt sorry for Elizabetta, and thought she was a fool not to see through him! She'll end up with his name, at least, and perhaps that's all she ever wanted.*

*But I was even more susceptible to him, even more of a fool when it came to his personal charm. And I wasn't even bright enough to strike a deal that lasted.*

Rod had pulled a chair around and sat down on it, his arms folded across the back, his eyes bright. "What's the plan, Heather? We can organize the neighborhood again."

"I don't know," the wrought-iron lady said. "If he's going to build something, it might not be so bad. I wasn't counting on selling him all those staircases anyway."

There was one thing obvious about the woman, Heather thought irritably. She was certainly flexible!

"It begins to look as if our activist group is shrinking, Rod," she said dryly. *But maybe,* she thought, *if we act promptly, Cole doesn't need to know that.*

She was stripping off her apron. "If I'm not back in fifteen minutes, Rod, call Cole and tell him I'm inside the school, and I'll be staying there."

"You can't get in," he argued. "Those aren't the pansy padlocks they used to lock it up with, Heather. It would take a battering ram."

"I'll find a way." It was grim.

"And all I get to do is sit here and wait?" he yelped.

A smile fluttered across her lips but didn't reach her eyes. "Of course not, Rod. You're running the command post."

He grunted a little. "How will I get through to him?"

"That's his private number, beside the phone. I doubt even he could have had it changed since yesterday. And Rod—no free samples to your friends."

She tossed her cap and apron into the kitchen and hurried up the hill. She was out of breath by the time she spotted the salvagers' trucks parked in an out-of-the-way nook beside the gymnasium wing, and their ladders propped against the side of the building.

Not a soul was in sight. She called, but there was no answer, only the unmistakable sounds of destruction coming from above her head, on the two-story-high roof of the gymnasium wing. There was the clank of roof tiles like pieces of china clicking together, and then a sharp-edged crash as a tile fell and shattered, followed by a muffled obscenity.

*Already they're causing irreparable damage,* she told herself. *If it's going to be stopped before it goes any further, it's up to you to stop it.*

*And the first step is to talk to those people on the roof.*

Just looking at the ladder made her dizzy, and she wished she had manned the telephone herself, and sent Rod up here instead. Or perhaps if she went back to Cookys and called a lawyer...?

No, she thought, that wouldn't be much use. It might be different if the building had been already registered as historic, but it was too late to pull that off, and Cole knew it. He was probably counting on it. By the time any action could be taken, the damage to the building would be too great to repair, and demolition would be the only alternative.

So if anything was to be done, it had to be now. And it would have to be Heather who did it.

She looked up at the ladder again. *Just take it one rung at a time,* she told herself, *and don't look down.*

The ladder was aluminum, and it felt insubstantial to her grasping fingers. The rungs seemed to bounce and bend under her feet, and she began to think as she climbed that walking over a bed of hot coals would be a picnic compared to this.

*I'm halfway,* she told herself reassuringly. *Surely I must be halfway by now!* But she didn't dare look down to check on her progress, and above her the ladder seemed to stretch up into the clouds.

Her head reached the level of the roof's edge, next to the slot where a stone gargoyle had once reposed. Had the salvagers already removed it? she wondered. Or had it been knocked down long ago? She could not remember.

Two more rungs, and she could swing her feet over onto the tiled slope of the roof, where another ladder was anchored. This one looked even worse, because of the unnatural angle of the climb. She stopped a moment to try to force air into her tension-constricted lungs, and wondered how people who worked in places like this ever managed to unwind when the day's work was done.

She kept her eyes firmly on the tiles directly ahead of her, and clenched her teeth.

*If I ever get down off this roof in one piece,* she told herself, *I'm going to drink a whole bottle of champagne to celebrate!*

The structure of the roof surprised her, for at the top of the second ladder she found herself standing perilously on a flat, tarred surface. "That's strange," she mused. "From the ground, it looks as if this wing has a peak that matches all the rest. It's an architectural trick."

One of the salvage men jumped up from the corner where he was prying off the top row of tiles, and spun around. "Lady, what the hell are you doing up here?" he sputtered. "This is not some kind of carnival ride!"

"I've come to supervise," Heather said lightly. "It's all right, I'm one of Cole Dennison's associates."

He grunted. "You've still got no business on this roof." He planted his hands on his hips.

Heather ignored him. She picked her way gingerly toward the center of the roof and did her best to keep from glancing back toward the edge. "So how long do you think it will take to tear it all down?" she said.

"Everybody wants a guarantee," he said sourly. "Who knows for sure?"

"You must have an idea. You can't do business without some sort of a plan."

He shrugged. "The beams in this place must be fifty feet long, some of them. If you don't get everything done in the right order, you'll pull the wrong one out first and the whole building will collapse."

The tiny flame of hope that had stayed alive in her heart—the hope that it might have been only the roof they were working on, and not the entire structure—flickered down to nothing and was smothered.

"And that hardwood flooring—take it up in a hurry and you'll split it into matchsticks. It all takes time."

Heather had stopped listening. *Everybody wants a guarantee,* she thought. Translated, that meant Cole was anxious to have the job finished. Well, that was no surprise; of course he would want to get his new construction started promptly, to take advantage of the season. And he would want to get this site cleared before there could be any legal challenge, and before the neighborhood could organize itself again.

And he would probably succeed, she thought.

"Now if your curiosity is satisfied, lady, how about getting off this roof?" The salvage worker was almost pleading.

Heather said absently, "Sure. I'll get off." She turned, forgetting about the vista she had been so studiously ignoring. It spread out before her in one incredible panorama—the valley with its retail district, the rolling hillsides full of suburban homes growing smaller as they receded and, beyond it all, in the hazy distance, the tall towers of the city's heart....

She staggered, and felt the too-familiar beginnings of panic. There was nothing between her and that distant vista to keep her from falling. And there was no way to escape, except to go back down those flimsy ladders. Coming up had been bad enough, but the mere thought of swinging over empty space in order to put her feet onto those vibrating aluminum rungs—

She tried to take a deep breath, but there wasn't room in her chest for it. It felt as if her lungs had anticipated what was coming, and collapsed so they wouldn't have to take part in it.

The worker was coming toward her. "Watch your step, lady!" he snapped. "It's not in the best of shape up here, and I don't want to be responsible if you fall through—"

"Joyful thought," Heather muttered. She had turned her back on the view, unable to bear it any longer, and her eyes fell on a metal fire escape at the corner where the wing joined the main section of the building. There must have been a lower section once that had led down from the gymnasium roof, but it had been removed—no doubt to help secure the building from trespassers, she thought, once there were no longer students who needed its protection. Now it only led upward, from the roof where she stood to the upper floors of the main building.

*Great,* she told herself. *You're afraid of heights, so you're thinking of going up even higher!*

But at least it was an actual staircase, with an actual handrail. No more ladders.

She flitted across the roof and up the stairs. All the salvage workers were screaming at her now, but she knew better than to look down through the metal grates that formed the steps.

At the very top of the fire escape was a door—locked, of course. But the window right beside it had never been covered with plywood, and the putty had long ago dried out and failed. When she put her hands against the glass, it tipped slowly from the sash and splintered on the hard floor inside. The opening it left was just big enough to let her crawl through.

The salvage men were right behind her. She put her head back out the window. "I'm only going to go down the inside way," she said breathlessly. "Don't pay a bit more attention to me."

The characteristic, familiar throbbing of a helicopter began to beat at the corner of her mind.

*Dammit, Rod,* she thought, *I told you to wait fifteen minutes! Now I don't even have time to think about what to do next—*

The red-and-silver bird was not yet in view. Frantic, she darted down the dark hallway, looking futilely for a place to barricade herself, and her eyes fell on the little closet that concealed the winding staircase that led up to the tower. By the time the helicopter swooped in over the building, she was climbing through the trapdoor.

She had forgotten the strength of the turbulence produced by the rotors, or perhaps it was stronger high in the air, where the bulk of the building couldn't act as a baffle. She ended up clinging to one of the pillars that supported the tower roof, her face pressed against it, until the helicopter had passed and a dozen irate pigeons had retreated to wait for the intruder to depart. She expected the pattern of the carved stone would be forever part of her.

By the time the helicopter settled softly into the school yard, she had managed to pry herself away from the pillar.

When Cole stepped down from it and stopped at a safe distance to look up, with his hand sheltering his eyes, she waved from her perch on the ledge that rimmed the tower. It was not the most comfortable of seats, but she had little choice in the matter; her knees had abruptly gone on strike.

She couldn't see Cole's face clearly, but she saw the shadow that crossed it when he saw her. She saw the abrupt way he held out his hand for an object—the key to the big front doors, of course. And she saw the way the other men with him scurried back toward the helicopter as if looking for cover, while Cole climbed the main stairs alone.

It was going to take him a while to reach her perch, she knew, so she leaned back cautiously against the corner pillar and whistled a little to keep her courage up, concentrating very hard on the tower itself, so she didn't have to look at the view beyond. The tower was bigger than she had expected—twenty feet square or so—far bigger than it looked from the ground. There were a dozen pillars; they were grouped at the corners to support the Gothic arch of the roof, so the entire center space was open. Every bit of stone trim was touched with elaborate carving. Why had they wasted the effort? Heather wondered. Who would ever see it up here?

She heard the trapdoor creak, and said, without turning her head, "Hello, Cole."

She watched him from the corner of her eye as he climbed onto the roof. He was approaching her very slowly—very cautiously—as he might have if she'd been holding a hostage over the edge. Or if she'd been preparing to jump.

"Don't worry," she said idly. "I'm not on a suicide mission."

He didn't even sound out of breath. "Is that supposed to relieve my mind?"

She shrugged. "I thought it might."

"The truth is, I was thinking about pushing you. Why in hell are you suddenly up here enjoying the view, anyway?"

"I thought if I came up here, you'd realize how very serious I am about this."

"Oh? I thought perhaps your whole afraid-of-heights routine was a put-on."

She spun around on the ledge to face him. "Why, you— Are you suggesting I pulled that stunt in the glass elevator on purpose?"

"The possibility had occurred to me."

"Well, it was not manufactured panic," Heather said stiffly. "I have a great many better things to do than plot how to get you to kiss me!"

He moved across to the opposite ledge, set a foot up on the edge of the stone and looked out across the valley. "I wish you'd make up your mind, you know. First you don't want to talk to me—now all of a sudden you do."

"I didn't have anything to say, before."

"And now you do? So what is it, Heather? And why didn't you just use the telephone?"

"I am trying to make a point," she said stiffly. "You promised, Cole. You gave me your word of honor that you wouldn't destroy this building."

He shook his head a little, but it was not a gesture of denial, she thought, which surprised her. It looked more like confusion.

"Of course," he said. "It would be this damned building. Nothing else matters to you. What's the problem?"

"You expected me to just overlook this little twist in the plans? You know, it really doesn't matter if it's bulldozers and wrecking balls that knock it down in hours, Cole, or hand tools that take weeks or months. Why don't you just do it with dynamite and get it over with in seconds? You could put a charge right here in the tower—it would be quite a sight to see it explode—"

"Heather, I'm not tearing the building down."

"Do you think I can't see? Or that I'm stupid? The salvage people were honest, at least." She waved a hand in the direction of the gymnasium roof. She couldn't see it from here, but when she wasn't speaking she could hear the screech of nails being released from the wood they had held fast for decades, so she knew the men were back at work.

He folded his arms across his chest. "What did they tell you?"

"Why don't you just give me your version," she said coolly, "and let me be the judge of whether the stories match?"

He muttered something under his breath that she was glad she hadn't quite heard. "I don't know why I bother," he said. "That wing was added forty years ago, Heather, when the main building was already half a century old. They did a fair job of matching the original section in appearance, but the construction is much inferior. Add the damage from the fire, and it's a mess. It isn't structurally sound, and it never could be made so again. We're stripping off the wing, that's all. And the salvage people are doing it so the tile and brick and stone can be reused." He rose, and strode across to the trapdoor. "Next time, DeMarco, get your facts straight before you make a fool of yourself."

She sat there stone-silent on the ledge for an eternal moment while the truth sank in. The salvagers were on the site, talking of flooring and beams and tiles, and so she had thought they must be demolishing the entire building. It had been a natural assumption to make—but it was completely wrong. Cole was not, after all, tearing down the school in order to use the land for some new project.

"But I *do* have my facts straight," she said stubbornly. "Audrey told me you're planning new construction for the site. Or do you expect me to believe you've conveniently changed your mind in the half hour since I talked to her?"

He stopped with one foot at the edge of the trapdoor. There was tension, wary watchfulness in every line of his body. "Audrey talks too much. What else has she told you?"

Heather raised her chin defiantly. "What else is there to tell me?" she countered.

Something flickered in his eyes. "Nothing that matters." It was very quiet, and before she could wonder about it, he went on. "Yes, there will be some new construction. She's working on the plans now for several small buildings to be added behind and off to the sides of this one."

Heather frowned. "What on earth for?"

"Apartments. Four- and six-unit buildings, small enough to blend into the landscape and not detract from the school. By renovating this building and adding new ones, we'll have a variety of housing, and enough units to support an on-site manager and an indoor pool and all the extra amenities."

"Apartments," she breathed. "You found a way to do it! Oh, Cole—" She jumped up and started toward him, hands outstretched.

"Anything else you'd like to know?" he said coolly. "No? See you around then."

She watched, unbelieving, as he disappeared through the trapdoor and down the stairs.

*Get your facts straight before you make a fool of yourself,* he had said.... Well, she'd done a prize job of making herself look like an idiot this time, that was sure. What had she thought she was proving, anyway? she asked herself tightly. This was just another stupid stunt—one more in a whole collection! Breaking into his office, making that announcement at his party, falling in love with him and dreaming of happily-ever-afters—they were all stupid stunts. And now this one—accusing him of lying, without even giving him the benefit of the doubt. Accusing him because it was a way to see him again, if she were to be painfully honest about it. *What did you think would happen, Heather? That he'd be so glad for the chance to see you that he'd...*

Tears blurred her vision, and she didn't see the rough edge on the tower floor, where the flagstone block had broken. But she felt the sudden emptiness under her foot. As she fell, a nightmarish picture flashed through her mind—the image of herself sliding helplessly down the steep roof and over the edge, into infinity—and she began to scream.

She smacked into a hard surface with an impact that jolted her entire body, and for an instant she lay there, eyes tightly closed, afraid of what she would see if she opened them.

"Heather," said a hoarse voice, and a hand came roughly to rest on her hair. "Heather—my God, I thought you'd gone over the ledge."

She dared to open her eyes, and saw only the flagstone floor of the tower and the knees of a soft gray suit, where he had dropped to the floor beside her. "So did I," she said shakily.

There was no strength left in her, and when he helped her to sit up and put his arms around her, she turned her face weakly into his shoulder, and thought that if she only could, she would stay there forever.

His mouth was pressed against her temple, and the contact seemed to burn straight through into her brain, paralyzing all the logical circuits and leaving her mind to float.

"I'll take you home," he said huskily.

"No—" It was an automatic protest. "I'm still a little shaky. I think I'll stay right here for now."

His hand passed softly down over the tangled length of her hair. "I never should have left you up here, knowing how afraid you are."

"No," she whispered. "You shouldn't. You never should have left me at all." *But you did,* she thought. *You left me for Elizabetta. And that changed everything.*

He had pulled back from her, and he was looking at her quizzically.

Hastily she said, "I'll be fine. Go ahead, Cole. I can get myself down from here."

His arm slipped slowly away from her. "You're not going to give me another chance, are you?" He sounded almost sad. "I wish I understood what changed you, Heather. You were the most beautiful, most loving, most giving woman in the world that night—even through your tears. But when morning came, you sneaked away from me as if you were ashamed of what we'd shared."

"I didn't want to wake you," she said stiffly.

He shook his head. "It was a whole lot more than that. You looked at me as if you were appalled at seeing me there in your bed, and you would have stolen out of the apartment if I hadn't followed you."

"You can't know how I looked at you," she said uncertainly. "You were asleep."

"No. I was waiting till you came within range, and I was going to pounce on you—until I realized that you and I weren't playing the same game anymore. Why, Heather? What happened?"

She drew up her knees against her chest and folded her arms around them. What harm could it do to tell the truth? she thought. At least then he would have to accept her answer, and leave her alone. And perhaps, then, she could start to heal.

"Because it was only a game," she said drearily. "And I found I didn't like the rules anymore." She tried to laugh. "Oh, it's not your fault, Cole. You did your best to make things clear. It's silly of me, I suppose, not to want to share. But now that you and Elizabetta have had your talk, and reached your understanding—"

"Heather," he said between clenched teeth, "you said you didn't want the damned house!"

She pulled away as if he'd suddenly sprouted horns and started breathing fire. "How did the house get into this?"

"You said you hated it, so I offered it to Elizabetta for exactly what I've put into it, just to get rid of it in a hurry. And if you—"

"You offered it—" She had to stop and swallow hard. *"You sold her the house?"*

"Yes. And if you tell me now that you want it back, so help me God, DeMarco, I *will* throw you over that ledge!"

"You didn't—ask her to marry you—again?"

He sounded as if all the air had been knocked out of him. "You thought I had?"

She nodded. "It was the only thing I could think. You said you had to talk to her, now that she'd had a chance to think things over. It was perfectly clear that everything you'd been doing was to try to get her back, and—"

"Clear to you and your crystal ball, maybe," he growled. "Dammit, Heather, you can't think I still wanted to marry Elizabetta!"

"You were engaged to her—until I messed it up. Love doesn't die overnight like that, Cole, because of a stupid misunderstanding."

"You're right," he said. "Love doesn't die like that."

Her heart sank slowly to her toes, and beyond.

"But when it was never really love to begin with—that's different altogether."

"Then . . . you didn't love her?" Heather whispered.

He shook his head. "I liked Elizabetta well enough," he said quickly, as if it was a lesson he'd learned and he was determined to get through it as soon as possible. "And I felt sorry for her, too, because she didn't have an easy time of it with Jack Winchester. I never pretended it was any grand passion, and she didn't, either, but there wasn't anyone else I was particularly fond of, and we were alike—outsiders, both of us—and it just seemed to make sense." He sighed and pulled Heather close, until her head fit neatly under his chin. "But when you came into my office that day, like an unexpected breath of spring air—"

"You went ahead with your engagement party," she reminded him.

"Yes, I did, because I didn't think you could possibly be real. Women like you just don't exist, Heather. And all my reasons for marrying Elizabetta were still there. Then you showed up at the party, and I discovered that my breath of spring air was really a cyclone—"

"I'm sorry about that."

"No, you're not, so don't lie to me. When I got back into the ballroom after sending you home, Elizabetta didn't even question what was going on. When I asked her if it bothered her, she just said that she had been away for a long time, and of course she understood that these things happened."

"And that made you wonder what she'd been up to in France, I suppose?"

He frowned. "Funnily enough, that never crossed my mind. I just thought it was because of the way Jack had treated her—he had a reputation for that sort of appetite. But I told her I thought we should reconsider the whole thing."

She pulled away and looked up at him in surprise. "*You* broke it off? Not her?"

He nodded. "You see, till then I really thought that she was marrying *me*—not my position or my money. But when I looked at that cold-blooded woman and realized that she honestly didn't care what I'd been doing while she was away—"

Heather sighed. "I've treasured that image of her, you know. Shredding your character in hysterical sobs."

"Elizabetta would never allow herself to be reduced to hysterics. Just as she would never rub her nose while she thought things over, or get the sniffles after crying—because she never cries. And she would never demonstrate for a cause or crash a party, either." He was watching her closely. "And she would absolutely never lick her lips like that. It drives me crazy to see you do that, Heather."

"Oh? I didn't realize I was doing it, actually. I'll try to stop."

"Not that kind of crazy." He pulled her against him once more, very closely. "*This* kind of crazy."

It was a long and deep and satisfying kiss; it left her body trembling and her mind in shivers at the idea of how near she had come to sending him out of her life altogether.

"You could have told me," she said, and reached up to stroke his face, delighting in the feel of his skin against her fingertips.

"I suppose I should have. But I wasn't sure enough of myself right then to want to say much of anything. I don't mean to sound conceited, but I've been a target for a long time. I've seen a lot of feminine acts in my day, Heather, and I wasn't sure for a while if yours was just a particularly good one. And don't forget I was nursing a few bruises over not having seen through Elizabetta earlier."

"When did you conclude I was real?"

"When you kept telling me you hated the house, and made me believe it—made me look at it through your eyes. It wasn't until the day I listened to you and Audrey rip the place apart that I realized how bloody awful the whole thing was."

"I know," she said. "Once you'd relegated it all to Elizabetta, you didn't even think about it anymore."

He nodded ruefully. "At any rate, by the time I was certain of the way I feel about you, I guess I'd simply forgotten that you might still have the wrong idea about Elizabetta."

"The way you feel about me?" she whispered.

"I love you, Heather, and I will love you forever. And I want you beside me—as my wife."

He could read her answer in the light in her eyes, and before she could find words to express it, he had drawn her close again. It was a good while later that he said, "One thing we must agree on, Heather—we've had too many secrets, and too much grief because of them. There must be no more unanswered questions, and no more hiding fears and thoughts and feelings. Honesty is the ground rule. If we want to know something, we ask. All right?"

"All right," she said demurely. She laid her head against his shoulder. "Cole... what else was Audrey not supposed to tell me?"

He released a long breath of amusement. "Dammit, Heather, you'll ruin all the surprises. Come downstairs, and I'll walk you through your new apartment." He stood up and pulled her easily to her feet.

"Here? In the school, you mean?"

"Well, there isn't room in the brownstone. And we can't live in the hotel suite or we'll both be nuts within weeks. We could get an apartment at Dennison Tower, I suppose, and just keep the curtains closed all the time, but I thought this was a lot better solution, since the penthouse here is only on the fourth floor."

"The penthouse," she mused.

"Nearly all the time you've been working on the château, Audrey's been picking your brain for what you really like, and putting it all together here. We'll even have a place to hang the potted geraniums."

"We will?" she said doubtfully.

"The tower, of course." He waved a hand expansively. "This is our patio. We'll put a barbecue up here so I can grill hot dogs for you on Saturday nights."

"Cole, you idiot!"

"I just got the floor plans yesterday. I was going to bring them over last night to show you."

She shook a finger at him. "Remember what we said about honesty, Cole? You were at the Century Club last night with Elizabetta."

"No. I was going to go—after you'd made it clear I wasn't welcome in your life anymore, I decided it was stupid to dangle around like a glass ornament on a Christmas tree, so I was going to go on with my life. But at the last minute I decided not to go. I sent my regrets, and my resignation, and told them there were other charities I'd rather fund."

"Cole! You'll be thrown out of society."

"I doubt it. I'd have a lot more fun at old-time street fairs in Archer's Junction anyway. Do you suppose we could get them started up again?"

"I think you could do anything you wanted."

"Remember that," he ordered.

"I love you," she whispered, and for a long time they didn't talk at all.

Finally he raised his head. "Heather," he said unsteadily, "you asked a question once that I've never answered—what am I going to do about your baby?"

It took effort to pull herself back from the edge. Her insides were like ice cream on a summer afternoon—slick and shimmery and shivery-cold.

"I will love it," he whispered. "Very nearly as much as I love you. And as for all the fuss about who your baby really belongs to..."

"Yes?" It was only a breath.

"Don't worry about it anymore. All your babies will be mine, too. And they won't be illegitimate, because you're going to marry me very soon...."

Then his mouth came down gently on hers in an endless kiss, and she answered him the only way she could.